Jack Approache With A Gentle Touched Melanie's Heart. "Look What We Made, Melanie."

He leaned down to kiss the top of his daughter's head.

Melanie's heart melted just a little. She'd been alone with Juliana so long that sharing her with Jack felt strange...and sweet. She hadn't known what to expect from Jack Singer, Navy SEAL, but watching him fall in love with their daughter in less than a second wasn't it.

He looked at Melanie, his gaze moving over her with the same intensity as it did with their child. "I'm here. I'm staying, and I'm in her life whether you want it or not."

"I know."

"You don't like it."

"Nope."

"I think you've forgotten why we came together in the first place." Jack brushed his mouth over Melanie's. She tried a retreat, but he wrapped his arms around her and held tight until she responded to his kiss.

The instant she did, he drew back.

"Expect me in your life, Melanie. Constantly." He grinned. "Daddy's home."

Dear Reader,

This season of harvest brings a cornucopia of six new passionate, powerful and provocative love stories from Silhouette Desire for your enjoyment.

Don't miss our current MAN OF THE MONTH title, Cindy Gerard's *Taming the Outlaw,* a reunion romance featuring a cowboy dealing with the unexpected consequences of a hometown summer of passion. And of course you'll want to read Katherine Garbera's *Cinderella's Convenient Husband,* the tenth absorbing title in Silhouette Desire's DYNASTIES: THE CONNELLYS continuity series.

A Navy SEAL is on a mission to win the love of the woman he left behind, in *The SEAL's Surprise Baby* by Amy J. Fetzer, while a TV anchorwoman gets up close and personal with a high-ranking soldier in *The Royal Treatment* by Maureen Child. This is the latest title in the exciting Silhouette crossline series CROWN AND GLORY.

Opposites attract when a sexy hunk and a matchmaker share digs in *Hearts Are Wild* by Laura Wright. And in *Secrets, Lies and...Passion* by Linda Conrad, a single mom is drawn into a web of desire and danger by the lover who jilted her at the altar years before...or did he?

Experience all six of these sensuous romances from Silhouette Desire this month, and guarantee that your Halloween will be all treat, no trick.

Enjoy!

Joan Marlow Golan

Joan Marlow Golan
Senior Editor, Silhouette Desire

Please address questions and book requests to:
Silhouette Reader Service
U.S.: 3010 Walden Ave., P.O. Box 1325, Buffalo, NY 14269
Canadian: P.O. Box 609, Fort Erie, Ont. L2A 5X3

The SEAL's Surprise Baby

AMY J. FETZER

Published by Silhouette Books

America's Publisher of Contemporary Romance

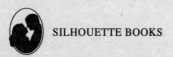

SILHOUETTE BOOKS

RECYCLED PAPER · RECYCLED PAPER

ISBN 0-373-76467-7

THE SEAL'S SURPRISE BABY

Visit Silhouette at www.eHarlequin.com

Printed in U.S.A.

Books by Amy J. Fetzer

Silhouette Desire

Anybody's Dad #1089
The Unlikely Bodyguard #1132
The Re-Enlisted Groom #1181
*Going...Going...Wed! #1265
*Wife for Hire #1305
*Taming the Beast #1361
*Having His Child #1383
*Single Father Seeks... #1445
The SEAL's Surprise Baby #1467

*Wife, Inc.

AMY J. FETZER

was born in New England and raised all over the world. She uses her own experiences in creating the characters and settings for her novels. Married more than twenty years to a United States Marine and the mother of two sons, Amy covets the moments when she can curl up with a cup of cappuccino and a good book.

For Rhonda Pollero, Cherry Adair and Maureen Child

Our careers made us friends
Our support and love for each other made us sisters
Our circle is joined and powerful

ASPEN is just the beginning....

I love y'all.

One

Congratulations! It's a girl!

Still in his field uniform, Lt. Jack Singer blinked and read the postcard again. The card was a picture of an old plantation and he recognized his sister's handwriting.

"Hey, I'm an uncle. I have a niece!"

Jack's SEAL teammate, Reese Logan, smiled. "Great! Tell Lisa and Brian I said congrats."

A girl. Jack frowned. That was all she'd written. Odd for shutterbug Lisa not to send pictures. Odder still that his sister hadn't even told him she was pregnant. Not that she could have reached him by any other means than this post-office box. He'd been gone fifteen months on special operations, and no contact with the world beyond his commander and his team had been allowed. It was the toughest part of being a SEAL. Cutting ties, or letting them blur badly enough that people often forgot about you.

Melanie Patterson obviously had.

He flipped through the mail, not finding what he'd hoped. A letter. A message that the woman he'd spent a mind-blowing night with after his sister's wedding hadn't really dismissed him from her life. Closing his mailbox and pocketing the key, Jack strode to the command center, tapping the postcard against his thigh. He had thirty days' R and R coming and knew exactly where he'd spend it. He'd take the time to see his sister, his new niece—and maybe find Melanie and ask why the hell she'd cut him out of her life with the precision of a surgeon.

The reality hit him that maybe she'd forgotten about him.

Bad news, when all he could remember about his sister's wedding was Melanie. She'd been the maid of honor, Lisa's best friend and three years older. And the kind of woman who made men damned glad they were men.

Jack headed for the phones and dialed Lisa's number, realizing he should be more excited about his new niece than getting the chance to grill his sister about Melanie Patterson. That was a signal, Jack thought, he should be glad the woman didn't expect anything from him. But he wasn't.

When he'd managed to get near a ship-to-shore phone months ago and had clearance to call, he'd discovered Melanie's phone was disconnected. It was as if she didn't exist anymore. He'd phoned his sister and asked, but Lisa'd said she hadn't seen or heard from Melanie in months. He was worried and irritated at the same time.

Why wouldn't she speak to him? They were good together, in and out of bed, and Jack, sifting through junk mail, replayed that night in his mind for the millionth time. The memory of making love with Melanie was enough to drive him crazy, just as she had that night.

"No mail from her?"

Jack shook his head, listening to the ringing on the other end of the line as the SEAL team members stripped off their gear and turned the most expensive components into the requisition officer.

"Give up, pal. I got the message, even if you didn't."

Jack's gaze shifted to Reese. "SEALs don't give up."

"They fight the battles they can win, and the woman has made her feelings damn clear."

Jack shook his head, wondering why his sister's answering machine wasn't turned on. "Melanie Patterson is worth going after for a straight answer."

Reese smirked. "Grab a life vest, Lieutenant, because your ship's already sinking."

Jack scowled, more at himself than at his friend's words. He'd never really thought of himself as that far gone. Sure, he'd thought about Melanie a lot and wanted to hook up with her now that he was stateside again. Yet there was more to it. They'd connected in more ways than in bed, and he wanted to see her again to find out if that connection was reality or just the memory laced in fantasy.

* * *

Fifteen months earlier

The wedding was over.

In his late father's place, Jack had walked his little sister down the aisle, given her to the man she loved and, as of a few minutes ago, put them both into a limo and sent them off to start their life together. His mom was off with her friends. Now he could focus on the object of his torment for the past two weeks.

The maid of honor, Melanie Patterson. Just being near her was enough to make his mind fog. He didn't want to think about what she did to the rest of him. He'd been fighting it for more than 336 hours. Since he'd first laid eyes on his sister's best friend.

He'd suffered through about forty snags in what he considered a well-thought-out plan for his sister's wedding, yet through it all there was Melanie. Calming Lisa, running errands and running Jack ragged.

Leggy, opinionated and so damn sexy he thought he'd burn up with his need to touch her.

When he wasn't fixing a problem that threatened to ruin his little sister's big day, he was with Melanie, talking to her long into the night, sailing on the river with her when they could grab a moment from the chaos of the wedding. When she wasn't near, he was thinking about her, waiting till he could get the sassy redhead someplace private and dark. And find out if she tasted as good as she looked. He'd bet a month's pay she did.

He wasn't alone in this. He knew that for certain, or he'd have mentally shut down his libido and kept far away from her. They were subtle, the hints coming from her, and caught him dead in the chest. They made him want her even more.

As the limo rolled away from the officers' club, he waved to his sister and looked at Melanie. She was holding the hem of her gown, bending down to pick up a ribbon-tied pouch of birdseed. The officers' club wouldn't let them throw rice, and Melanie had convinced them that birdseed was environmentally safe. She only wanted the tradition for Lisa, she'd said. No bride should leave without the wish of prosperity from those who loved her.

And no man should have to stand here, look at a woman like that—and behave. "Melanie?"

She looked up, smiled, then straightened. "Hey, Lieutenant. Did I tell you how very dashing you look in that white uniform?"

"You can start now."

"A Navy SEAL with an ego," she teased. "How rare."

He held out his hand for hers. She dropped the pouch of birdseed into it. He glanced down, then stuffed it into his pocket.

"Sentimental?"

"No, I'll have the bills to remind me of this."

She laughed and said, "So, the cynic emerges. I knew you weren't all patience and knightly duty."

Around them, the caterers began cleaning up. The band still played one last song, and while the guests departed, Jack pulled Melanie into his arms and onto the dance floor.

"You looked great this morning."

"As opposed to right now?"

He smiled. She kept him on his toes, he'd give her that, and found himself wanting to give her a hell of a lot more. "The belle of the ball."

"Thank you, and I won't tell your sister you said that."

He pulled her more firmly against him, and the single touch of her hand in his, her body to his, set off fireworks under his skin.

She inhaled a soft breath. "Jack." She tried to ease back.

"Shh," he murmured, sweeping her across the dance floor like a duke at a summer ball. "You feel it, don't you?"

"Oh, yeah," she breathed, and held on to him, laying her head on his broad shoulder.

He loved it, the feel of her; she fit perfectly in his arms. And he knew they'd be a perfect fit elsewhere. "Good. I was hoping I wasn't in this torment alone."

"Not a chance, sailor." Her arms tightened around him, her hands moving up his back in a heavy caress.

He wished they were on his skin. Wished the two of them were naked and rolling across his bed. "You've been driving me crazy, you know," he whispered close to her ear, and sent gooseflesh cascading over her skin.

"You'd never know it."

"It wouldn't be nice to go after the maid of honor while Lisa was falling apart over those flowers, would it?"

"You're to be commended for your restraint, then, Lieutenant."

"With what I've been thinking about, I should be court-martialed."

Melanie lifted her head from his shoulder. Her gaze moved over his handsome features and understood the message she saw there. Heat, hunger. Need. She'd been receiving it for more than fourteen days.

Jack Singer had walked into Lisa's living room amidst yards of tulle and satin, and one look had struck Melanie with the force of charged lightning. It wasn't so much that he was good-looking, which he was, or that his naval uniform fit like a glove and the sight of him in it would make any woman weak-kneed. It was his eyes, eyes that shouted his emotions, as well as hid them from the world.

She remembered the way he'd looked at Lisa this morning, in her gown, the picture of a fairy princess, and she'd seen those deep-blue eyes gloss with tears. Of love and pride. Who'd have thought such a strong man with a dangerous job could melt at the sight of a bride? But just as easily, she recalled the stare he'd delivered to the florist who was going to ruin his sister's big day, and the words "If looks could kill" came to mind in an instant.

"What have you been thinking?" she asked suddenly.

"Dangerous territory," he warned, his blue eyes smoldering as they raked over her.

"I'm up for the adventure."

"With me, right now?"

She slid her arms to his shoulders, the fingers of one hand sliding up the back of his neck and tipping his head down. It was as if she'd done it a hundred times before, as if she'd known him for a thousand years.

"I was wondering when you'd get busy," she whispered, and pulled him closer. His mouth covered hers, devoured with savage need as his hands climbed up her satin-covered spine and crushed her to him.

It was all-consuming, as he'd known it would be. Hot and fast and too private to be seen in public. His body was hard, hers firm and yielding against his.

"Whoa, Singer!" he heard from somewhere in the distance, and he pulled back. His breathing was hard.

"Can it, Reese," he said to his buddy without taking his gaze from Melanie's.

"Sir, yes sir," came the response.

"Let's get out of here?" The words came like a question.

She blinked and licked her lips. "We aren't gone yet?"

He smiled and let her go grab her purse. Then they rushed from the club. During the cab ride to the hotel, he didn't touch her, didn't kiss her, not trusting himself if he did. He only held her hand. It was the most erotic thing he'd ever done. Fingers laced, palms tight. Intimate.

More than he'd been with any woman in a very long time.

At the hotel he climbed out of the cab, paid the driver and took Melanie's hand again as they entered the building and stepped into the elevator. He couldn't look at her. Her body was still imprinted on him from the dance.

He still felt her warmth. Smelled her scent. It was eating him up inside.

People smiled and nodded. A man mentioned being in the Navy during the Gulf War, and Jack hoped he made the proper respectful response. People got on and off and the elevator kept moving. Slowly,

slowly. Then, finally, they were alone, the only ones in the elevator shooting to the top floors. He couldn't stand it and turned toward her.

She smiled, reaching for him at the same time, and when he backed her up against the wall, he kissed her like a madman.

And she answered him, clinging, her mouth hot and wild beneath his.

Jack felt himself fracturing inside. She grasped his hand and put it on her thigh, under the slit in her gown, and Jack groaned, driving it higher, feeling the stockings, then skin. He cupped her buttocks and wedged her closer. Little soft sounds came from her, and he wanted to hear more, hear her cry out with pleasure.

Then he dipped his hand between her thighs, rubbing.

She gasped, her fingers digging into his shoulders as he stroked her. She broke their kiss, whispered, "This is so naughty."

And he said, "Yeah, I know. I'll never forget it," then hooked the edge of her panties and pushed a finger deep inside her.

"Oh, Jack," she said, bowing away from the wall, gasping for air.

Jack toyed with her, a single fingertip sliding over slick, soft flesh. Her panting breath tumbled from her lips and filled the elevator. He introduced another finger.

"Oh, my!"

"Oh, *yes*," he growled, kissing her throat. She was wet and slick and tense against him, tuned for the explosion. Then the *ping* of the elevator made them draw apart, both moaning in disappointment. He muttered a curse and when the doors opened, grabbed her hand and damn near ran to his room. The hall was empty and he fumbled with the key card.

She took it, met his gaze, then inserted it in the slot. The door sprang open and he dragged her inside, kicked it closed and pushed her against the door.

She laughed at his impatience and he kissed her. Deep and heavy and thick. She popped the buttons of his dress white jacket and kicked off her shoes. He toed off his own and shrugged out of the stiff coat. Then she turned around, her hands braced on the door. Jack pulled the zipper of her satin dress down. His eyes flared and his body tightened when he saw the matching lavender bra and panties. He laid kisses down her spine, taking the dress with him as he did, and when it was a pile on the floor, he turned her around and looked his fill.

"Man, oh man," was all he could say.

She arched a brow and unhooked her bra. His gaze raked her, his breathing quickened, and he stripped off his T-shirt.

She grasped his wrists and placed his hands over her breasts. Jack didn't need encouragement. He was ready for her now. Had been ready for this for two long weeks.

Each time he'd brushed against her, electricity shot through him.

Each time she'd smiled or laughed, he felt alive and rewarded.

He rubbed her breasts, his palms brushing over her nipples. They hardened and he couldn't wait to taste them. Then he did, taking one nipple into the heat of his mouth and sucking deeply.

Her leg lifted, her foot sliding up his calf.

Melanie felt her world tilt and shift. Pleasure radiated outward from her breasts, singing through her like music, making her blood run fast and hot and to the rhythm of Jack's touch. He nibbled and licked and her nerve endings grew taut. His teeth scored, his tongue soothed, over her breasts, her ribs and lower.

Deliciously lower.

He caught his thumbs in the sides of her panties and drew them down as he sank to his knees. He touched and kissed her legs, hands smoothing down to her toes, then back up. Then he hooked her knee and drew it over his shoulder.

He met her gaze. She smiled, running her finger over his lips.

Then he tasted her. And everything she knew shattered.

"*Jack,*" she groaned softly.

His tongue plunged and laved and flicked, and she cried out, wanting more. She was greedy for this man. Greedy for everything she could get because she more than liked him, much more, and she knew he would leave, knew he'd disappear into the mist. A quiet warrior. It was his job, his life. There was only right now. And she wanted all he had.

And he gave it, finding and teasing every sensitive pulse point, every bit of flesh that was charged and waiting for ignition. He lit the fuse and she burned. Oh, how she burned!

Jack felt it, the spiral of heat racing through her,

the tightening of her muscles, the liquid softness of her desire. He spread her wider and thrust two fingers inside her.

Desire exploded, shuddering through her, clutching at him.

"Jack!" she moaned. And he wanted to hear more, wanted to be the only man she did this with, wanted to be the one she shared herself with. A possessiveness he'd never known rose in him.

He didn't ignore it. But he didn't need it. Couldn't encourage it. Not when he might be a thousand miles away from her in a few hours. So he savored the moments, the small and big ones, as he had for years, as he would for the next decade.

He took her past her climax, beyond madness and satisfaction, and back into his world, his arms.

He stood and she fell against him, limp for a moment, only a moment. Then she kissed him and fire kindled as she reached between them to unfasten his belt. She shaped him, the bulge in his trousers, then pulled the zipper down. His hands braced on the door beside her head, he smothered a groan as her fingers dipped inside his trousers and freed him.

"My turn."

"Nah-ah."

"What's the matter, Lieutenant—running out of steam?"

"No, afraid of launching without a target."

She laughed and increased pressure, stroking him wildly and pushing his trousers down. He kicked them aside, pulling her flush against him. The impact of flesh to flesh left them shuddering, weak.

His hands mapped her body, stroked and dipped,

and he wasn't the only player. Her touch taunted him, made him grow harder, and he scooped her into his arms, then strode to the bed. He set her in the center and she pulled him down, opening for him, eager for him to be inside her.

Skin met skin and he held her, wrapping her in muscle and man, and Melanie thought, *Never in my life has it been this perfect.* When he reached for the end table, she took the condom from him.

He arched a brow.

She grinned and pushed him onto his back and straddled his thighs. Jack sat up. She pushed him down, then opened the packet and drove him wild as she rolled it down.

"Melanie! Sweet mercy!"

"I don't think so," she said, and shifted to straddle his hips.

He grinned, loving her openness, and cupped her breasts, leaning up to take her nipple into his mouth.

Melanie forgot almost everything when he did that. "Oh, Jack, you do that so well."

"Yes, ma'am."

She smiled, kissing his face, then rose. "My hero."

He guided himself into her, and she held on to his shoulders, meeting his gaze as she sank down. He filled her, thick and throbbing. Jack experienced more than the feel of this woman around him, of being so deep inside her. But he didn't understand it. He tipped his head back and she smoothed hair from his brow, let her fingertips stroke his face.

"Melanie—"

"Shh," she said. "Not now." She saw it, the connection that went deeper than sex. All wild and hurried eagerness was gone. The rush had died to a sweet poignancy. They had to have each other. It was as if pieces were missing and here they came together. Joined. One.

She moved, releasing him and taking him back, claiming a man she could never have. He was a mustang. Free. Noble.

And she wouldn't dare try to tie him down. Or ask him to stay. Though she couldn't bear the thought of losing him when she'd only just found him.

Two weeks was not enough. Yet in his eyes, in the eyes that could be cold as ice and tender as a lamb, she saw more. More than he could give. More than sex.

Jack grasped her hips, his gaze never leaving hers as he gave her motion, never leaving hers as he pulled her down onto the bed beneath him and pushed deeply into her.

Her legs trapped him and he went willingly into the snare.

Her heart beat against his and he danced to the tune. Sinking. He withdrew and plunged, and she rose to greet him, to take him into her and into her soul. And when feminine flesh gripped him in a slick glove, pulsing as he pulsed inside her, Jack knew he'd relive this night a thousand times in the future. And want it never to end.

He pushed, long deep strokes that brought cries from her, brought pleasure in mounting waves. Their tempo increased, bodies moving in a damp and primal rhythm, his gaze locked on hers and refusing to let go. Flesh throbbed and squeezed; he drove deeper.

Then it came, the hot prickling rush that fought the surface of skin and bone and erupted. Sensations folded in on each other, breaking apart and coming together in a blinding moment that hung for seconds, then minutes before releasing them.

He thrust hard once and final. A claim. He watched her green eyes darken, watched her smile bloom and felt warmth spread through him. She pulled him down onto her, holding him as the rapture faded.

She whispered his name in a throaty purr, then kissed him with a power he'd never felt before.

He knew then and there he'd never stop wanting her. And that the night wasn't over yet....

The phone rang at 0600 hours and Jack groped for it, knocking it off the cradle and then dragging it to his ear.

"This better be good, Reese." Otherwise, his good buddy was going to earn himself a black eye.

"Lieutenant Singer? This is Colonel Walsh."

Jack was instantly awake and sitting up. "Yes, sir."

"Plans have changed. Report ASAP."

"Yes, sir."

"How was the wedding, son?"

Jack's gaze moved to the slender bare back tucked against his thigh. "Memorable, sir. Perfect."

"Outstanding. See you in a few hours." The colonel hung up.

Hours. Damn.

Melanie turned her head and met Jack's gaze. "You have to go, huh?"

He nodded, sliding down into the bed and pulling her into his arms. She scooted on top of him, resting her folded arms on his chest.

"I knew this would come," she said, and her eyes teared. She was going to miss him. "I was just hoping for a few days with you."

He ran his hands over her naked spine. "Me, too."

She inched up to kiss him. "Don't ask me to wait for you, Jack. I don't know if I could stand not knowing when or if you'll ever come back."

"I'll come back and when I do, I want to—"

She shook her head. "Don't make promises you can't keep. I'm not."

"Why?"

"Because I more than like you." Oh, she was falling for him too fast, she thought. "And I can't put my hopes on a man."

Jack frowned softly, and realized he knew very little about this woman's past. But he could tell she'd been hurt. Badly.

Melanie wasn't going to cling to Jack, nor to any man. She'd been left alone with only her broken heart to hold more times than a woman should have to suffer. She had to go on with her life as if he'd never touched her heart so deeply, as if they'd never joined so intimately.

It was almost good that he was leaving so soon. Two more weeks of Lt. Jack Singer and she'd find herself hip-deep in love with him. And that was dangerous. And pointless.

He rolled her onto her back. "I'm not one of those guys—"

"Shh," she said, and spread her thighs, urging

him between. "Come to me, Jack," she whispered, and tried to keep her voice even. "Before you head to parts unknown for who knows how long. Give me all you hide from the world."

He searched her eyes. "Why?"

"Because I'll keep it safe." It was all she could offer.

He pushed inside her, losing himself in her, giving her what she wanted. All that he had.

And little did they both know, leaving a bit of himself behind.

Two

The front door swung open and Jack's sister glared at him. "Well, that's not the fine welcome I expected from my only sibling," he said.

"I'm wondering if I should claim you as my brother." Lisa made a sour face and spun about, striding into the living room. Jack stepped inside and reached for her.

"Hey, what's up? Bad day with the baby? Who I'm dying to meet."

"Really?"

"Hell, yes. Uncle Jack wants to pamper the little lady. My right, you know." He produced a stuffed koala bear.

Lisa softened a little, but not for long. She gestured to her house. "See any baby things around here?"

He looked. The little house she and her husband, Brian, owned was immaculate, homey and adult. He frowned. "I don't get it."

"I didn't have a baby, Jack."

He stepped back, scowling. "Then why did you send me that card?"

Lisa glanced to the side, avoiding his gaze, something she never did.

"Hey, darlin', what's going on here?" he said in the voice that always got her to share with him.

She looked at him. "I sent the card to get you to come home and face your responsibilities."

His brows shot up. "What responsibility?"

"The one to your daughter, Jack."

He paled. "I don't have a child. I'm not a father."

"Oh, yeah? Well, she's six months old and her name is Juliana. She has your hair and your eyes."

Jack choked on his own breath. A baby? There was a baby in this world that was his? His gaze snapped to his sister's. Reality slammed into his gut.

"Melanie. Where is she? I tried to call her."

"You called?"

He gave her a look that said, "Thanks for the vote of confidence," and he wasn't pleased about it. "Yes, I did—when I got to a ship-to-shore phone. I sent her a few notes while I was out at sea, but she couldn't write to me." His look said what he was doing with the SEALs wasn't up for discussion. "Still, when I got stateside, there was nothing, no phone listing, no address."

Lisa met his gaze. "You really called her, huh? When she said she didn't want you to know, I thought it was just a…well, that she was hiding her feelings.''

"Don't you think I had the right to know?''

"Of course! That's why I sent the card. Good grief, Jack, I thought you hadn't contacted her. That's the impression she gave me.''

"How did you find out?''

"Brian and I were in Charleston on a little vacation and I went into the bank to cash a check. Melanie was the bank manager. She's moved back here now, but she really doesn't want you in her life.''

"Well, she's getting me, dammit,'' he muttered, heading to the door.

"Jack, wait! She's not going to like this.'' Lisa moaned and folded her arms over her middle. "What are you going to do?''

"Talk to her, marry her, give my daughter *my* name. My child isn't going to grow up like I did, Lisa. I won't allow that.'' He let out a breath. "Tell me where she lives.''

Jack marched up the neat path to the little house. It was a perfect cottage in the woods, far back enough from the street to be private and surrounded by a small picket fence to protect a child from the traffic.

He stopped short. A child. His child. Good God. Melanie had given birth to his baby. Alone, without him. Without him ever knowing he'd become a father. And his daughter was already six months old! He'd missed everything. Missed seeing Melanie round with his baby, missed the baby's birth, those moments when dads go into complete panic with the coming of labor pains. He'd missed his baby's first smile, her mother's first look of pride... Damn. Inside, anger as wide as the Chechessie River warred with a strange feeling of absolute joy.

He was a father. There was a baby in that house that was half his. A life he and Melanie had created that night. And she'd tried to take that from him, take away his chance for something more than what he was.

Anger boiled and he continued to the door, knocking hard.

It flung open an instant later.

And his breath punched out of his lungs.

She looked incredible. More incredible than she had during those two weeks. His heart pounded like a hammer in his chest. His gaze ripped and dipped over her body. Jeans never looked so good on a woman. A T-shirt never looked so sexy. Red hair spilled over her shoulders, and if he hadn't been staring at her body he would have noticed the look of surprise and anger on her face.

Then he did. Well, so what, he thought. She was the liar. She was the one who'd denied him his rights to his own child. "I hear you have something to show me."

Her features yanked taut. "I'm gonna beat your sister up, just so you know." The day in Charleston when his sister had walked into her bank, her whole world had crashed. Melanie had been feeling so alone then, and seeing her best pal had opened a floodgate of anguish she hadn't known she'd held back. She'd missed Jack so much. Really missed him.

"Yeah, well. That won't compare to what I'm ready to do to you."

Her look was leery. "Perhaps you should come back when you've calmed down a bit."

"I am calm."

She arched a brow, trying not to let her heartbeat shoot through her throat at just the sight of him. "Try again, Jack. You look ready for battle."

He stepped closer and enjoyed her indrawn breath. "I'm always ready—it's my job. Or did you forget that about me, too?"

Melanie didn't forget a thing. Not the look in his eyes when he wanted her, not the one he got when he was mad. And he was furious. But then, she knew he would be.

"So are you going to invite me in or do I have to push my way inside?"

She didn't say anything, the inevitable too clear to argue. She stepped back, waved him inside and closed the door.

He stood close, looming over her, and Melanie wanted nothing more at that moment than the feel of his kiss. His arms around her. Seeing as that was dangerous, she went for reason. "I didn't try to keep this from you, Jack."

Her soft tone and liquid eyes caught him in the gut. "Then how come I'm the last to know?"

"I couldn't reach you. You're a SEAL." She moved into the living room. "Everything you do is top secret and cloak-and-dagger. I called your unit and spoke to an Ensign Frostbite—"

"Frostbite?" he interrupted.

"As in, his attitude was chilling enough to give me some."

Jack tried not to smile. She'd called, he thought, removing his cover and tucking it in his belt. She'd tried to contact him. Some of the fire went out of him.

"He said that since I wasn't your wife or next of kin, I couldn't speak with you. Even Lisa tried to contact you for me once, but no one was dying or anything, so they wouldn't oblige." She shrugged, understanding in the movement. "And well, tell him he's the father of a girl, eight pounds seven ounces, is not something you want to leave in a message."

She moved behind the sofa, dragged her fingers over the edge, tweaked a pillow, and for a split second he saw her as she was then, pregnant, hanging on to a phone and talking with a by-the-book ensign, wanting to tell Jack, but unable to reach him. "Yes, I guess not."

"I decided I had to wait."

"I called you a couple times and wrote. My letters came back unopened, undeliverable as addressed."

Something old and smothered in Melanie tried working itself out just then. "I'd moved home to be near my parents. But I'd always liked it here, so we came back." She wasn't going to admit to a soul that it was because of Jack. She'd survived fine without him. She'd had a baby alone, hadn't she? But then she'd moved back to this place, where she knew he'd be able to find her if he wanted. Real brave, she thought.

Jack glanced around at his surroundings. The interior had a sudden calming effect on him. While the furnishings were elegant—cherry tables, wing backed chairs—the fabrics were casual. Tiny checks and crumpled velvets in sage-green, cream and little splashes of maroon and emerald. Fat pillows with tasseled corners were strewn on the sofa and floor. Elegantly rumpled, he thought and realized he liked it.

Then he noticed the toys. His heart slammed into his chest as he bent to pick up a doll. He rubbed his thumb over the belly, the little gingham dress, and tried to imagine his child playing with it.

"Where is she?"

"She's sleeping."

He met her gaze. "I want to see her."

"I'm not waking her to see a stranger, Jack."

"I'm not a stranger."

"But to her you are."

"I won't wake her up. I just want to look at her."

"In a few minutes, okay?"

As long as she knew he wasn't leaving without a look at his baby. "So what did you tell your parents?"

"Nothing more than they needed to know." And once Juliana arrived they were the grandparents any child could hope for.

His temper quick-started like an engine. "Dammit. So they think I'm some sort of jerk that would let their daughter have a baby without helping?"

"No. They don't think that. They understood."

In truth, her father had been the hardest to handle, and given a moment of free rein, Dad would have turned over mountains to find Jack, punched his lights out, then make him marry her. Which was the last thing Melanie wanted.

She didn't want a husband because of a child.

But Jack was honorable, a real hero type, and though he hadn't gotten to it, Melanie suspected there was a bigger battle coming.

He folded his arms over his chest and widened his stance. "So, enlighten me. How did this happen?"

She sent him an innocent blinking look. "Gee, sailor, think maybe we forgot protection one of those times?"

"Don't get cute. That I figured. It happens. I was as willing as you were. I have no regrets." He arched a brow, the question unsaid.

She felt the heat of that night spin through her and light her from the inside out. She could almost fall into his arms again if he wasn't looking at her like a new target to assault. "Neither do I, Jack."

His stance softened. "Then if you accept that, why couldn't you accept that I would want to know, to help?"

"Other than I couldn't contact you," she reminded him. "I didn't need it."

"And that makes it right?"

"Maybe, maybe not." She moved to the kitchen and started preparing a pot of coffee. Maybe by giving up on hunting him down she thought she was doing him a favor. A man like him, with a dangerous job, he didn't need to be worrying about her and a child when he was supposed to be concentrating on keeping his head down and staying alive. Just the thought of him being distracted by her when he was in the line of fire gave her nightmares and kept her from charging into his unit office and embarrassing herself and Jack by demanding he be contacted. Then she just got used to thinking alone, doing alone. But all she'd wanted then, when she was round with his baby and wondering what he'd think, was to hear his voice.

Jack followed her and said, "What about what I needed, Melanie?"

She glanced over her shoulder. "And you needed a daughter?"

"How the heck should I know? I've never had one. And if it was up to you, I never would have known about her."

Melanie glanced toward the hallway. "Keep your voice down." She flipped the switch on the coffee-maker.

Jack moved to her, gripped her arms and stared down at her. "Talk to me, Mel."

He was hurt, she could see. More deeply than she'd thought.

"You kept my baby from me," he went on. "That's not easily forgivable."

"I did what I had to do, with the resources I had. You were unreachable. They wouldn't even tell me if you were in this country."

He hadn't been, but he couldn't tell her that. "Did you even once think of me?"

She blinked, hurt and insulted, and pushed off his touch, stepping back. "How can you say that? I had your baby growing inside me, Jack. All I thought about was you. When I was screaming in pain deliv-ering her, I thought about you and I wanted to beat you senseless, by the way."

She looked down, her throat tight. She'd been angry with him then, she remembered. Angry because he wasn't there to see his daughter being born, that he wasn't there sharing the responsibility thrust on her. But he was off fighting evil, being the hero, a higher purpose, she'd finally reasoned. And she'd just…accepted. Oh, she knew she should have never let this man touch her. Not because of Juliana, but because his touch left an imprint that went clear down to her soul.

"If I'd known, I would have let you."

"But the Navy wouldn't have. I know, having a child is no big deal in the military. Women do it alone all the time. But I knew that the first chance Lisa blabbed, you'd be here."

"And now that I am, we're getting married."

"Oh, so now it's ride-to-the-rescue Singer? Do I look like a damsel in distress?"

"You look like the mother of my child, and that child needs my name."

"Mine's been doing quiet well for me for twenty-nine years. It's good enough for her."

"Why are you being so stubborn?"

"I don't want a husband who would marry me for the sake of a child."

"Why? Is that so archaic to you?"

"Yes." And it's full of doubts to start with, she thought. She couldn't go through life, through a marriage, with him, a man she barely knew. And she didn't want to live with the constant uncertainty of does he want me for myself, or me because I'm the mother of his child? Or because it's the right and honorable thing to do? And Jack was up to his eye-balls in honor and duty.

Jack let her go, dragging his hand over his head, then his face. "You are about the strangest woman I know."

"Isn't that why we jumped into bed in the first place? Because I wasn't falling all over you like the other women?"

"No, it's not, and if you can't see that, then it's probably good that I wasn't around when you learned you were pregnant with my child."

"Why?"

"Because I would have made certain you knew the truth of my feelings for you, Melanie."

"You don't love me, Jack, so don't say it."

"I won't. It's not true."

Her heart fractured. Well, that was honest, any-way.

"But whatever it is I feel for you is strong enough that thoughts of you have been dogging me for months." He headed to the hallway and Melanie was still reeling in reaction to that.

"Excuse me? Where do you think you're going?"

"I need to see my baby."

"Jack, wait."

He stopped short, his features sharpening with an-ger. "I've been waiting. I've missed six months of her life. I'm not going to miss another minute."

A soft cry filtered from the hall and Jack froze.

"Now you've done it," Melanie snapped, then shifted past him and headed down the hall.

His temper defusing like a puff of smoke, Jack followed, but she was already out of sight. He listened for sounds, following them, and stepped into a small room decorated with pink and lavender fairies. But he wasn't interested in wallpaper and mobiles, but the woman who stood near a crib.

There was a coolness about her, a reserve that hadn't been there before. He could feel a wall neatly erected between them and she was doing her best to keep it strong. Was it to keep him from her or his daughter? Things were too brittle between them right now for Jack to make huge waves in Melanie's life, but he wasn't going anywhere. He was well-known in his unit for his patience, and he'd exert some of it now. Because she still set him on fire with just a glance, it was all he could manage not to grab her in his arms and kiss the living daylights out of her. His memory was damn good, and he pushed down the need to satisfy the hunger that had simmered for nearly a year and a half. Patience, he warned himself, his gaze sliding over her as she hung over the crib.

Everything in him went still as she reached inside. She lifted the baby, fat little legs pumping the air. The child squealed and Melanie held her close.

Jack felt his heart fill and explode at the sight of his daughter.

"Juliana," he said, and Melanie looked at him. "Lisa told me, and…" He gestured to the name in stuffed letters hanging on the wall and held by two pink fairies. He stepped closer, his gaze moving over his daughter. Round-faced and healthy, she had dark hair like his, eyes like his, but her beauty was all her mother's. Her head tucked under her mother's chin, she stared at him with wide eyes the color of cornflowers. Jack had never seen anything so beautiful. And he loved her instantly.

"Hey, princess."

Melanie watched Jack, the wariness she'd never thought to see in him coming to the surface. He faced bullets like most people faced the morning. But he approached his daughter with a gentle hesitancy that touched her heart.

"She's beautiful."

"Yeah," Melanie replied as he ran a fingertip along Juliana's arm. The baby simply stared at him, as if familiarizing herself with his face.

Jack moved as close as he could, their baby between them. "Look what we made, Melanie." He leaned down to kiss the top of his daughter's head, thinking she smelled of powder and innocence.

Melanie's heart melted just a little. She'd been alone with Juliana so long that sharing her with Jack felt strange...and sweet. She hadn't known what to expect from Jack Singer, Navy SEAL, but watching him fall in love with their daughter in less than a second wasn't it.

"I want to hold her, but I know I'll scare her," he said softly.

"She's still sleepy."

"I'm sorry if I woke her. I didn't think."

"It's okay," Melanie said, watching his eyes, the way he touched Juliana, as if coaxing her into accepting him a little bit at a time. Yet when his fingertips slid up Juliana's arm tucked against her mother, they brushed Melanie's breast. Heat ripped through her, and her breath snagged.

He looked at Melanie, his gaze moving over her

with the same intensity as it did with their child. "I'm here. I'm staying, and I'm in her life whether you want it or not."

"I know."

"You don't like it."

"Nope."

He arched a brow, stroking the top of Juliana's head and loving the sounds she made. "Then it's war, huh?" He tipped his head, catching Melanie's chin and tilting her face till she looked him in the eye. "I think you've forgotten why we came together in the first place."

"We were both randy."

The corner of his mouth curved. It scared her. He looked more dangerous at that moment than he would have if he'd been armed with an assault rifle and wearing camouflage paint.

"Yeah, sure." He brushed his mouth over hers. She tried to retreat, but he wrapped his arms around her and held tight. Their daughter fussed and gripped his shirt, one of his medals. Jack felt something new and strong rocket through him, and he increased the pressure on Melanie's mouth, molding her lips to his, and wanted to shout when she responded.

The instant she did, he drew back. She was breathing a little harder, her eyes a little glassy. Victory loomed on the horizon, he thought. He had to have patience for the long journey. "Expect me in your life, Melanie. Constantly." He grinned. "Daddy's home."

He looked down at Juliana, touched the top of her head and suddenly knew this little girl was the best part of his life. Yet knowing Melanie was like a lioness protecting her cub right now, defensive and distrusting, Jack didn't try to take his child into his arms. Yet they fairly ached to hold her, to feel her little body against his chest, hear her heart beat.

Instead, he said, "I'll see you both real soon," then spun around and left the room.

Melanie gripped the crib rail. Because her knees had melted. Her heart had stopped. She looked down at Juliana. The baby gurgled, and blew bubbles.

"That was Daddy. What did you think?"

Juliana jerked in her arms and smiled.

"Yeah, he does that to women. He's going to be a real pain, honey. What are we going to do?"

Her daughter didn't offer a solution and Melanie didn't have one, either. All she knew was that Jack Singer could turn her inside out and upside down with a glance. And with a kiss…oh, she was useless.

But she wasn't going to marry him. So it would be best just to keep him out of her life completely. Big talk, she thought, when just now his presence turned you into a puddle. Well, she wouldn't let that happen again, nor would she give him any ideas that she'd agree to marriage. Going into a marriage with such low expectations wasn't her dream of a future. She had a future. She and Juliana would be just fine.

Part of her dreaded Jack's showing up again. And he would. She might not know a lot about the man, but one thing was for sure. He'd drawn a battleline in the dirt and she was scared of the first attack. Because Lt. Jack Singer, Navy SEAL and handsome as the devil, was a gentleman.

His attack would be subtle. But she didn't doubt that when it came to something he wanted, he'd fight dirty.

Three

———

Jack drove his sports car around town for an hour with no destination in mind. He thought about calling his buddy, Reese, then decided that he didn't want anyone ever to get the wrong idea about Melanie or his child. Not like they'd had about him when he was a kid.

His fingers tensed on the steering wheel and he pulled up to his hotel and shut off the engine. He didn't get out, his mind tripping over plans, over ways to get into his daughter's life.

And into her mother's.

Man, he thought, rubbing his face. Melanie Patterson didn't look like a mother. He didn't think it was possible for her to look better than she had that night after the wedding. But she did and her kiss was just as hot. IIc tried to imagine what it had been like for her, tried to imagine her belly swollen with his baby, and when he did, something sparked inside him. Longing?

Did he want *in* her life because of the baby?

He checked that thought off the list in an instant. He'd done nothing but think about her for months. For fifteen of them. Being unable to talk to her all that time was like salt in the wound. She'd moved to live with her parents, sure, and her number here was unlisted, but the time wasted gnawed at him. He sighed. It wouldn't have changed much. Hell, he would have gone nuts if he'd known she was carrying his child, anyway, he thought. He'd have wanted to be there. With her, for her. He'd have done anything for that chance, and with his job, that just wasn't possible. He couldn't walk out when his commander called. When his teammates and his country needed him.

But dammit to hell, he hated that he'd missed it all.

Sighing with resignation, he left the car and headed up to his room. He didn't notice the women offering smiles as he passed. Didn't notice the way they tried to get his attention. All he saw was Melanie holding his daughter to her breast, stroking Juliana's little spine. He'd wanted to take the baby in his arms, feel the responsibility. But he didn't have to touch the baby to know it. It was already inside him.

Juliana was his daughter. His flesh and blood. And he was going to give her everything he'd never had. And that included her daddy's name.

* * *

Melanie looked at Lisa. "I know you're sorry. Forget about it."

"Well, you should have tried harder to tell him," Lisa said insistently. "It would have been easier if he'd known from the start."

"Yeah? How so? Would he have been any less…determined?"

"My big brother's a handful, huh?"

Melanie rolled her eyes. Her sorority sister was a romantic. Melanie wasn't. She'd given that up after her fiancé broke their engagement. Once was hard enough, but to be dumped twice? Melanie had a stellar record, falling for men who seemed to find the right girl after they'd already proposed to her. It was humiliating and the reason she didn't ask a guy for promises. They couldn't keep them. Jack wasn't any different. Well, maybe a little. He knew the meaning of honor, at least.

When she had been with him all those long months ago, women had flocked around him. She didn't want to see that he'd ignored them and focused only on her, but still. He'd had a few lovers before her. Lisa had mentioned them once or twice. Heck, any man who looked like a brick wall of muscle in Navy whites would have females young and old dropping at his feet.

Okay, so she'd been one of them. She'd wanted Jack. She'd always want Jack. He was under her skin, in her blood, whatever, but he was there. Fifteen months of trying to pry him out of her mind hadn't done much good. She still wanted him. Yet, in her bed was far different than in her life.

The phone rang and Melanie rose to get it. The

familiar voice on the other end of the line made her smile. "Mom, how are you?"

"Oh, we're fine. How's my granddaughter?"

Melanie smiled at her daughter sitting in her high chair. "Eating cereal and making a mess on my kitchen floor." Her mother laughed. "So what's up? I just talked to you yesterday."

"That was before Jack called."

"What?"

"Yes, just a little while ago. He talked to your father."

Melanie groaned and leaned against the wall. "And Daddy said what to him?"

"I don't really know. I know he was happy when he came out of the den, because he was laughing. He was still on the phone with Jack and took it with him out into the garage. Apparently your father and Jack hit it off. Did you know Jack makes furniture?"

Oh, great. Her father made furniture, too. The man had every tool ever made for woodworking, and now that he was retired, he produced more than her parents or Melanie had room for, so he'd branched out into taking special orders. And now it seemed Jack and Dad had bonded. Swell.

"Furniture, huh? No, I didn't know Jack made furniture." She glared at Lisa as if it was her fault that her father and Jack had things in common. Melanie asked to speak with her father, but he was out. "Ask him to call me, please, Mom."

"I don't think he'll tell you what they said—he wouldn't tell me."

Well, that was devious, Melanie thought. "Jack's

hoping to butter up you and Dad to get to me." She paced, her fingers tight on the receiver.

"Oh, he didn't do anything like that, sweetie. He just introduced himself and told us what we already knew. That he hadn't known about Juliana till now."

"What else?"

"He said that he would take care of you and his daughter."

"Well, Jack Singer is going to learn that I don't need his financial help."

Her mother's voice held a smile as she said, "I don't think he was talking about money, sweetie."

The words sent a trickle of fear down her spine. What was he up to? Melanie said goodbye and hung up, then sat back down and cupped her coffee mug. She'd sulk if she had the time, she thought, feeling a little betrayed by her parents.

"He called your father," Lisa said, her eyes wide. Melanie nodded. "Oh, gutsy Jack. That must have been interesting."

A little smiled twitched at Melanie's lips. "I bet it was."

Lisa pushed Juliana's cereal loops within reach. "You know my brother is a great guy, don't you?"

"I plead the Fifth."

"Hey, he hasn't done anything wrong."

Melanie sighed. "Except threaten me."

"What?"

"He said he was in my life and I couldn't stop him."

"Well, that is a threat, though weak and understandable." Lisa made faces at Juliana and the baby imitated her. "What are you going to do?"

Melanie shrugged. When it came to Jack Singer, she felt pretty helpless.

"You know, Brian's asked me to join him on his next business trip. For a month. I think I will."

Melanie arched a brow. "Jumping ship on me?"

"No, I'm trying really hard to preserve what I have. A wonderful friend and a loving brother. I don't want to have to choose."

"Who says you'll have to?" It was Lisa's turn to look doubtful. And darn it, Melanie could see her friend's point. She didn't want to put Lisa in the middle, either. "Okay, go. I can handle Jack."

Her friend stood and grabbed her purse, hitching it onto her shoulder. Lisa kissed the baby and smiled at the mother. "Good luck." She headed to the door.

"Why did you write and tell him?"

"Because as much as I love you, I love my brother best." Her eyes hardened.

So like Jack's, Melanie thought.

"What if that night was all we had, Lisa?" Melanie called when Lisa reached the door. She couldn't afford to get her heart crushed again.

Lisa looked at Melanie, sympathy in her eyes. "You have to give the relationship a chance to find that out, don't you, Mel?"

Before Melanie could argue that she had to risk an already bruised heart to do that, Lisa slipped out. Turning to her daughter, Melanie picked bits of cereal out of her hair and watched her bang her pudgy palms on the high-chair tray. There was no mistaking that Juliana was Jack's baby. She had his eyes. Intelligent, probing blue eyes.

"Hey, Jules," Melanie said, and the baby looked

at her, smiled brightly and offered a fistful of squishy cereal loops. Smiling, Melanie leaned down for a pretend bite. "I love you, munchkin. God, I love you."

Melanie blinked back tears and wondered what would become of them. She'd had it all figured out till Jack showed up. She liked things neat and in order, to know the outcome of events. Which was why she was a banker. Figures didn't lie. Figures didn't cheat on you while you were selecting china and bridesmaids. Numbers didn't leave you with the pitying gazes of everyone you had to tell about the broken engagement. Twice.

She wondered what was wrong with her that men left so easily. She was nice. She had a good sense of humor. She wasn't a supermodel, but she wasn't ugly. What was it about her that sent men running to someone more interesting?

Jack's face loomed in her mind as she gathered up her baby. She held Juliana closely and prayed Jack would just leave. She'd handled Craig's betrayal with his old love. She handled Andy's with his bimbo secretary.

But with Jack? If he got her hopes up and dumped her, well, she'd never recover. She was certain of that. And she'd have his daughter to look at every day to remind herself of her failure. No, it was better her way. No chance, no heartache. Right?

She looked at the baby. "Right?"

Juliana didn't answer. It was just as well. There wasn't one, she thought. There just wasn't.

Juliana was fussing for her dinner, Melanie was trying to get a load of laundry collected and into the washer before she started the evening phase of her day. Her day off, too, she thought. A heavy knock shook the door and for a split second, Juliana stopped whining and looked with Melanie at the door.

"Probably a salesman again," she said to her daughter, and crossed the living room. Propping the laundry basket on one hip, she opened the door.

"Jack."

"Good, you didn't forget me."

Like that would ever happen, she thought. Just looking at him made her insides turn to mush. "Why are you here?" Her voice sounded steady, right?

"Lisa and Brian took off and I was alone and hungry."

"Good that you have a houseful of food, because Lisa is a great cook."

Jack's gaze slipped over Melanie. She filled out those jeans better than any woman he'd known, but her face showed signs of fatigue.

"Then I guess you aren't up for takeout?" He held up the pints of Chinese food.

Melanie inhaled the delicious scent and smothered a groan. *Moo goo gai pan.* Her favorite. He fights dirty, she thought. "No thank you, we're fine." Juliana took that moment to exercise her lungs and Melanie glanced at her daughter. "Hey, be patient. It's warming."

"What's warming?"

"Her dinner, her bottle, followed by a bath, quiet time, then sleep."

"Then you get to do what, Melanie? Sit here alone and watch TV."

She made a rude sound. "I get to keep cleaning, working. Ironing my clothes for work. Then I get to rest."

"It's tough alone, isn't it?"

Her spine stiffened. She walked right into that one, she thought. "I manage. And will continue to do so, without your help."

"Hey, I'm not taking over, darlin', I'm just bringing chow." She arched a brow. He calmly gazed back, then smiled. "You going to keep me standing out here all night for the neighbors to see or what?" When she just stared, he swung the boxes. "It's hot. And I'm starving."

Tempting...so tempting. Both Jack and the dinner. But if she let him in now, he'd only expect to be able to come back whenever he felt like it. "So go home and eat it." She was too tired to deal with him now.

"Listen, Melanie, she's my daughter, too, and I barely got a chance to look at her."

A tiny twinge of guilt poked at her. "She has all ten fingers and toes, is in perfect health, and the longer you bug me, the madder she's going to get about being denied her dinner."

Jack pushed his way inside. "Then I guess you should hop to it, huh?"

"Jack."

"Have dinner with me, Melanie. We need to talk."

It was the smell of *moo goo gai pan* that did it, she thought. Not that smile. Not that pleading look she'd never seen on his face before. Okay, he was right, they needed to talk. Getting it all out on the table, so to speak, would make it clearer to Jack that she couldn't marry him.

She nodded and he smiled, walking to the kitchen and dropping the pints and bags on the kitchen table. She was right behind him.

He turned and took the laundry basket. "I'll do this."

"I'm capable."

"I don't doubt that. But Her Highness looks like she's working up to a Mach 1 scream."

Melanie looked. Juliana was trying to move the walker, but her legs were still too short and all she did was kick the air in frustration. The baby was reaching for her and Melanie's heart shifted. She handed over the basket and went to her daughter. "Come on, munchkin, dinner's on."

Jack watched her with the baby for a moment. How Melanie soothed Juliana, offered her a cracker as she set her in the high chair. She held a conversation with their daughter as if they were the only two people in the world, and feeling like the odd man out, Jack disappeared into the garage with the laundry basket, assuming that was where the washer and dryer were located. They were. He separated a load. Ignoring the lace panties and bras, he focused on the baby clothes. Baby detergent, he thought, remembering a TV commercial for it. He started the load and went back into the kitchen. Melanie was feeding the baby.

Jack watched. He couldn't help it. Just the sight of them, doing something so ordinary, fascinated him.

Then Juliana leaned out to look past her mother at

him. His heart soared and he blew her a kiss. She smiled and spit food as she tried her best to talk to him, and Melanie turned to look at him, a smile tilting her lips.

"I think we're communicating," Jack said.

"That doesn't say much for your intellect."

His gaze narrowed. "You're crabby."

"I'm sorry. I'm a mother. This time of day we're required to be crabby."

He smiled, shaking his head and moved to dish up the Chinese food. "You ready for some chow?"

"I'll wait. But you go ahead."

He frowned at her over his shoulder.

"I have to give her a bath after this. She sleeps better."

Jack nodded. "I'll wait for you. But…" He fished in a bag and took out a few egg rolls, then cut them in pieces and brought the plate to her. "Appetizers?"

She snatched up a piece and popped it into her mouth. Jack sat adjacent to her as she finished off the plate while she fed the baby. Then she cleared the dishes and lifted Juliana out of the high chair.

"Bath time," Melanie said to Juliana, then looked at Jack. "We'll be a little while."

A direct hint for privacy, he thought and leaned back in the chair and folded his arms. He wanted to be a part of their lives, not a pest. "I'm not going anywhere."

"Dang. Hopes dashed again," she said, and walked to the bathroom.

Jack shook his head. She was as determined to keep him at a distance as he was to get closer. But then, she really didn't know him that well. But she was going to learn.

A half hour later, Melanie closed the door to Juliana's room and stepped into the bathroom to clean up the mess in there. She was beat. And she really didn't want to deal with Jack on top of that, she thought, bending to collect dirty clothes and towels. She caught a glimpse of herself in the mirror and groaned. Her hair was coming out of the ponytail, she didn't have on a stitch of makeup, and her shirt had baby food all over the shoulder.

Some "I can handle everything" impression, she thought. She dumped the clothes in the laundry hamper and slipped into her bedroom to run a brush through her hair and change her blouse. It smelled, anyway.

When she stepped out of the bedroom, the aroma of *moo goo gai pan* made her mouth water and she walked toward the living room. Something more than maternal instinct made her pause at her daughter's room. She heard Jack's voice, soft and deep, like the distant rumble of thunder. Gently she pushed open the nursery door.

He was leaning over the crib, stroking the baby's back. "No, I swear to you, princess, nothing is ever going to hurt you. I'm here for you, even if Mommy doesn't want it. I'm not going away. And I'm going to protect you. You can count on it."

Melanie's throat tightened.

"I'll slay your dragons for you, princess. I give you my word of honor."

Tears burned in Melanie's eyes.

"And if she'll let me, I'll slay Mommy's, too."

Melanie swallowed hard and tried not to notice the flutter of her heart. Quietly Jack lowered the side of the crib and bent to kiss Juliana's soft brown curls. The night-light illuminated his features, fierce, and loving.

Her daughter had a champion, Melanie thought, backing out of the room. Whether she wanted it or not. But that didn't mean she had to like it. And it didn't mean she had to marry him just because he wanted it. She and Juliana had done just fine without him. She slipped into the living room and sank onto the sofa. She didn't want to doubt herself, her capabilities.

When he came out, he paused at the edge of the hallway, his hands on his hips. Tipping his head back, he took a long cleansing breath and let it out, smiling as he did. He hadn't noticed her yet. He looked as if he was measuring himself against the responsibility of fatherhood. She understood that. The day she'd learned she was pregnant with his child, she had done the same thing.

He met her gaze, like an arrow shooting straight toward a target. "Hi."

"Hey," she said. Lord, he was devastating to look at, she thought. In fitted jeans and a black T-shirt that flowed over every contour of his chest and arms, she wanted only to run her hands over that body. A body she'd had only one night to learn.

He moved toward her and her heart skipped an entire beat at that sexy hip-rolling walk of his. Did the man even know how powerful he was? Maybe he did, she thought as he slid down onto the sofa beside her.

His face was inches from hers, his gaze making a slow prowl of her features, the neckline of her blouse. Her breasts tightened in instant reaction.

"You keep looking at me like that and we won't be dining on Chinese takeout," he said softly.

"I'm starving," she said, and knew she should have kept her mouth shut.

"Me, too. But I'm only hungry for you."

Melanie felt herself turn to mush. "Jack, don't."

"What? Don't be honest? Don't tell you how many times I've thought about you?"

"This isn't helping."

"Denying isn't helping," he said, and leaned closer, his mouth a fraction from hers.

She could feel his breath on her lips. Almost taste him. And if memory served her, and it did, he tasted great. She leaned, and an instant before his mouth crushed hers, the phone rang.

She lurched to get it before it woke the baby.

"Hello," came out on a croak and she had to clear her throat. "Oh, hi, Michael."

Jack's blue eyes narrowed dangerously, and Melanie thought that between her disappointment at the interruption and the stupidity of falling into his arms again, this was the bucket of ice water she needed.

"Busy? Well, actually I am." She didn't look at Jack. "Sure. Bye." She hung up.

"Who was that?"

"A friend."

"How close a friend?"

She didn't mistake the edge to his voice. "I work with Michael."

"Was he asking you out?"

"I imagine he was trying."

"You'd date this man?"

No, she wouldn't. It would be trading one piece of heartache for another. But she couldn't resist asking, "Any reason I shouldn't?"

"Yes, I can barely get you to sit still long enough to speak with me and we have a child together."

And you're more dangerous to me than Michael could ever be. She could barely recall the guy's eye color, but there wasn't a thing about Jack she'd forgotten. "What is it that you want to say, Jack? Except propose marriage."

"You're not even going to consider it, are you?" he said.

"No, but thanks for the offer."

"You act like I did this without thinking first."

She folded her legs under her on the sofa. "It was a gut reaction, Jack. An obligation. I will not be a man's ball and chain when he doesn't want it."

"Who says I don't?"

"If Juliana wasn't between us, would you have come here first?"

"I've been in-country for three days and two of them I've been here. What do you think?"

"You want to do the honorable thing. I can understand that. But I don't need you to. Nor do I want to marry a man only for the sake of a child. Marriage is tough enough without going in with such low expectations."

"I don't have those—you do. I'll be a good father."

"Oh, I know you will," she said gently. "But you don't have to marry me to be one."

Jack thought of his own blood father. The man didn't marry Jack's mother, wasn't there for Jack when he was young and impressionable. Later, his mom had fallen in love with a great man, David, and they had married. Lisa was the product of that love, and the man Jack called Dad had been great to him, even when he didn't have to be. But Jack resented that his birth father hadn't the guts to marry his mother and left a little lost kid to bear the reaction of being a bastard. He would never do that to Juliana. Even if things didn't work out between him and Melanie, he was in his daughter's life for good.

He thought about telling Melanie his reason for wanting to marry, though he knew his father's lack of backbone was only part of it. Melanie herself was the real reason, and she wouldn't understand. She'd tell him that just because he was born out of wedlock didn't mean he had to make up for his father's mistakes—which was true.

Jack just didn't want to repeat them. Not at his child's expense.

Four

___

Melanie pushed through her front door, glad to be home. Her feet ached, and her head was brewing a whopper of a headache. Mostly because while managing the bank, she'd been plagued with thoughts of Jack and what happened last night.

She'd fallen asleep on him. Literally. And during a conversation she should have been paying strict attention to. This morning she'd awoken in her own bed, alone, the doors tightly locked and the dinner mess cleaned up. And no sign of Jack.

Jack at night was hard to handle.

Jack in the morning would just bring back a ton of memories of waking up in his arms, feeling his strength surround her.

She hadn't set her briefcase down before the scent of something wonderful cooking hit her full force and made her mouth water. Had Diana, her sitter, cooked? It wasn't unusual since the older woman did more than just care for her daughter.

"Diana, you shouldn't have gone to the trouble."

"I didn't, dear," the woman said before Melanie stepped fully inside the kitchen. "It's his show."

Melanie went still with anger. "Jack."

"Yes," he said, his back to her while he stirred something in a saucepan.

"What are you doing here?"

He tisked, keeping his back to her. "And here I was hoping our daughter got her smarts from you." He seasoned whatever was simmering in the saucepan and only glanced back briefly, throwing a beautiful smile in her direction.

It landed on Melanie like a blanket, warming her to her toes. How did he do that? she wondered. She bent to kiss their daughter, her gaze going to Diana.

While Juliana made excited noises, her sitter looked uncomfortable and said quickly, "He came over earlier to be with Juliana."

"It's all right, Diana. I'm sure Jack bullied his way in."

"On the contrary, he didn't want to come in till you came home, and we called the bank, but you were out."

"I was at the head office most of the day in meetings."

"And he is the child's father."

Question laced Diana's voice, and Jack looked back over his shoulder as if waiting for Melanie to deny that. "Yes, he is. But this is my home, Jack."

"And my daughter's."

"I didn't invite you here."

"She did. Isn't that right, princess?" he said, turning from the stove to lean down to the baby. Juliana grabbed his face and rubbed his nose with hers.

Melanie's heart dissolved in a puddle at her feet.

Jack flashed Melanie another smile that lit her insides like Christmas morning, then rushed back to the stove.

Well, this was a news flash, Melanie thought, fighting her smile. A U.S. Navy SEAL was at her stove, with an apron tied around his waist and looking awfully comfortable for a man who was more at ease wielding a machine gun than a spatula. With a quick glance she noticed the table was set beautifully for two; Diana was enjoying a cup of coffee and Juliana was in her high chair, gurgling at her father and chewing on the end of a wooden spoon.

Diana rose and set her cup in the sink. "I'll see you in the morning," she said, moving to the back door.

"Diana, you don't have to leave so soon." That sounded too much like a plea, even to her own ears.

Over at the stove, Jack chuckled.

"Oh, honey, yes I do," Diana said with a glance at the table setting.

Melanie rolled her eyes and waved the sitter off. That grin of Diana's spoke volumes. "Are you trying to seduce me with cooking?" she asked Jack after Diana was gone.

He looked at her. "No, but if that's what it'll take to get you to relax around me again..."

"I am relaxed."

"Then why are your hands in fists?"

"Because I want to pummel you for coming into my home without asking me."

"I tried. You should keep your pager on."

"The battery died this morning." She kicked off her shoes and went over to Juliana, lifting her out of the high chair and cuddling her close.

"I'm on leave, Melanie. I had all day to do nothing while my daughter was here with a baby-sitter. I just wanted to get to know Juliana."

She couldn't argue with that. Tipping her head to the side, she watched him. His ease in the culinary department was a bit of a shock. "I didn't know you could cook."

"There's a lot you don't know about me." His tone said he'd planned to change that. He poured steaming pasta into a strainer. "I have a lot of time spent just waiting around for the go ahead, so I read."

"Cookbooks?"

"Any book that's handy, to be honest. I don't get the chance to cook for more than myself very often, so grabbing this chance seemed like a good idea."

She rose and moved to the counter, careful to keep the baby away from the stove in case of splatters. Jack chopped fresh herbs, then lowered the temperature on a roux and stirred. The scents dancing through her kitchen were fantastic.

Melanie snatched a sample of the chicken he had cooling while he worked on a sauce, popping the chunk into her mouth. "Oh, man."

"Good?" he asked with a quick glance.

"Incredible."

"Why don't you change and get comfortable? I

fed Juliana already.'' As if he read her mind, he showed her the empty baby-food jar.

She took a step away, then paused to look back at him. He moved in her kitchen as if he'd been there before, and worked with great care, she noticed, dipping to taste, season, stir. But the fact that he was here, inviting himself into her life, her home, said that Jack wasn't going to be pushed out. If he was here for Juliana, she'd never deny him, but Melanie had a sneaking suspicion he had a plan she'd have a tough time to fight.

But right now she was so hungry she'd have gnawed through shoe leather, so if he wanted to cook, let him, she thought.

''Go on, Melanie. Have some time with Juliana.'' He didn't turn to look at her, and his ability to sense her like that was unnerving.

She headed to the bedroom with Juliana and couldn't help but notice how the baby gurgled loudly for Jack as she went.

Jack knew he was being a little devious, but with the way Melanie had reacted to him yesterday he knew she'd try her best to keep him out of her life. He wanted in. He told himself it was to see his daughter, that he'd already missed too much of her life and needed to catch up. But the truth was, there was more to it, and it had everything to do with Juliana's mama. He added a splash of water to the sauce and thought about how Melanie had looked when she arrived; businesslike, confident and sexy in that snug-fitting blue suit. He wanted to peel it off her and see what she wore beneath.

He marshaled his restraint and kept focused on

dinner. He wasn't trying to impress her. He didn't think his culinary skill made a difference to Melanie, but the fact that she didn't have anything in her freezer made him assume that she probably didn't do anything more than open a box and hit "express cook" on the microwave, and she hadn't been doing much for herself lately.

A half hour later, he heard her footsteps in the hall again just as he was popping the cork on the bottle of wine.

She stopped near the table, the baby on her hip. "I didn't have any wine."

"You didn't have much of anything. Jules and I went shopping."

"You took her out?"

"Yes, in my car, in the car seat, with Diana. Good grief, Melanie." He looked insulted.

"Sorry, I just haven't had to trust anyone with her except Diana in a while."

"I know." He offered a smile and a glass of wine. She thanked him, sipped and made a pleased noise as she moved toward the windows facing the back-yard. In soft cotton leggings and a lavender linen blouse she looked delectable, her deep-red hair spilling over her shoulders and catching the setting sun. Juliana was growing sleepy, and she rested her head on her mother's shoulder, her tiny fist wrapped in Melanie's hair.

Jack felt a swell of something close to pride when he watched them for a moment. Melanie whispered to the baby, rocking her gently. She'd already bathed Juliana and dressed her for bed. Jack didn't want his daughter to be sleepy. As far as he was concerned, he'd missed six months of seeing her grow.

Melanie set the glass aside, holding the baby closer, rubbing her back.

"Hungry?" he asked.

"Yes."

When she went to put the baby down for bed, Jack came to her. "Not yet, please."

"Have you ever tried to eat with a child on your lap?"

"Guess I'm going to learn." He took the baby from her.

Melanie's heart did a flip when Juliana curled against him with a contented sigh. They sat and Jack held their daughter, encouraging Melanie to eat while the food was hot. She tasted the meal. It was heavenly.

"Whoa. Okay, you're hired."

He chuckled and Juliana lifted her head to stare at him. Wide eyes skimmed his face, as if trying to understand who he was and why he was here. He smiled, kissed her, and satisfied with that, she laid her head back down on his shoulder.

Jack thought that nothing in this world would ever touch him as deeply as feeling his child in his arms, accepting him.

"Aren't you having any food?" Melanie asked.

"My mom said if the cook goes hungry, there's something wrong with the food. I will. I just don't want to give up my hands right now."

Melanie smiled. The baby looked like a pink dot against his wide muscled chest; his hand spanning the baby's back nearly covered her completely. Juliana's pink pajamas left fuzzies on his navy-blue polo shirt, but he didn't seem to care.

He held Melanie's gaze and whispered softly, "I love her already, Mel."

"I know," she said, and felt a catch in her throat. "I can tell."

It was good, too, she thought. He could have ignored her completely and never shown up, never wanted to see his child. It would have been hard to explain later on to her daughter, and it certainly would have made Melanie hate Jack. But that wasn't what she wanted. He was welcome to be with his daughter.

He shifted the baby into the crook of his arm and reached for his fork. Juliana opened her eyes briefly, then feeling safe, closed them. The man has already charmed his daughter, she thought, because Juliana was rarely content to just sit by while the world went on around her. She always wanted to participate in it, investigating her surroundings, tasting lint and paper, but her daddy made a difference. They had a rapport.

The realization should sting, since Melanie had been doing all the work since Juliana had arrived. But it didn't. How many times had she imagined Jack holding Juliana? How often had she wished he'd been here to share those first growth spurts, the day the baby could hold a cup, feed herself.

Tears burned Melanie's eyes and she focused on the meal. She didn't want to feel like this, confused and needing. She wanted to feel independent and in control.

Jack ate, but he could tell something was wrong

with Melanie. She wouldn't look at him and she barely said a word.

"Well, since I can't talk about my work, why don't you tell me about yours?"

She looked up, blinking, and he saw the trace of tears and frowned softly.

"I manage a bank." She shrugged. "And I'm a troubleshooter for two others. It keeps me busy."

"What about this guy who called, Michael?"

"He manages one of the other branches."

"Do you want to date him?"

"No, Jack. I don't want to date anyone."

"So you're going to close yourself off because you have a child?"

"No, I don't plan to, but she's young and she needs me right now." Melanie smiled at her daughter. "I'd rather be with her than out on a date any day."

Jack released a breath. He could understand that. Being with Juliana was more pleasurable than anything. His gaze snapped to Melanie. Well, almost anything, he thought, then tried to cut the chicken marsala using one hand.

"Can I cut that for you, or do you want to put her in her bed now?" Melanie asked.

He handed her the knife.

Melanie rose up a bit to help, laughing as she said, "I imagined doing this for her, not you."

"I bet you didn't imagine doing anything for me."

Her hands stilled before she went on cutting. "That's not true."

"Really?"

"Let me ask you something. What would you

have done if you learned I was pregnant *when* I was pregnant."

"Come home and married you."

"I thought so. But you couldn't come home, so we'd still be just like this. In this situation."

"I'd have convinced you to marry me."

"No, you wouldn't have. It has nothing to do with you, the man. It's me." She pushed the plate closer to him.

"Tell me, then."

"I can't marry a man for the sake of a child."

"I know, low expectations, which is garbage, but you and I...we're good together."

"In bed, yes."

"It was more than that."

She didn't answer. She couldn't let herself believe that or she'd be helpless around him, and she was already trying to deal with her need for him. "I don't know." She'd made mistakes before and didn't want to repeat them. She had her daughter to think about now, and what she did affected her, too.

"So you just shut me out?" he said.

She sighed, fingering the stem of her wineglass. She watched her movements. "Don't make promises you can't keep, Jack."

"And how do you know I can't? It's the job, isn't it."

"No, it's not that." He was gone for long periods of time, and usually even his family didn't know where he was.

"My daughter needs my name."

"But her mother doesn't."

"Dammit."

Juliana fussed and Jack stood. "I'll put her down," he said when she reached for the baby. "At least give me that." She nodded. He was gone for only a few minutes and Melanie sipped her wine. She could hear him and was tempted to go look, to check if he'd covered the baby, then somehow she knew he would. She just knew. Jack wasn't a man who did things halfway.

When he came back she was exactly as he'd left her, twiddling, moving food around her plate. He was pushing her and couldn't help it. The longer his daughter didn't have his name, the angrier he grew. He tried to see reason but one look at his child, he couldn't. Juliana would suffer for being illegitimate, even if her mother wouldn't. Juliana would know what it was like to be ridiculed through no fault of her own. She would be on the receiving end of the judging looks. Jack recalled one day when he was about seven and how he'd hitched a ride with a neighbor to his baseball game, and while all the other boys had dads cheering them on, he'd been alone because his mother was working her tail off to provide him with food, clothes and a decent place to live.

Other kids came from single parents and did fine, but it was the stigma of being a bastard that stung. Kids teased and often were ugly about it.

He refused to put his own child through that.

Jack went to the stereo and pushed in a CD, then came back to the table. He didn't say anything as he let the music soothe the rough edges.

"I'll back off, if that's what you want," he said.

Melanie's head jerked up.

"I'll stop pestering you to marry me." For now, he thought, since they were butting heads like two bulls. "But I want to be in Juliana's life and on *that* I'm not budging."

Melanie's gaze locked with his. She nodded. "Okay."

"Good."

"Why don't you come over during the day?"

He was well aware of the ploy. Be here when the sitter was and not when Melanie was. "You're setting limits?"

"No, it's just that—"

"Can't handle being me near, Melanie?" he interrupted. "Afraid you'll like it?"

"Of course I can handle it," she said.

"Outstanding. Because I have two months' leave and this is the only place I plan to be."

Two months, she thought. Oh, no.

He leaned back in the chair, chewing his dinner, and then grinned. Melanie looked nervous already. This was going to be interesting, he thought, and poured her more wine.

Jack was true to his word. He didn't mention marriage again. But he was being a nuisance. Melanie couldn't turn a corner and not find him near. And now this was going too far. He was at the doctor's office when she'd arrived, waiting for her. He wanted to see who was caring for his daughter and butted into the examination, asking a dozen questions. That was fine. He was Juliana's father.

But Juliana had to have one of her regular shots, and when the baby cried, Melanie cried, too. The nurse left them and Jack slipped his arms around her, holding both of them close.

"She's so little and I'm letting them hurt her," Melanie said.

His smile was filled with tender humor. "No, darlin'," he said softly. "She has to have them, you know that."

"I know, I know. I just don't want to cause her any pain."

The baby still cried and Jack lifted her from her mother's arms, holding her tightly and rubbing her tender thigh. He murmured to his daughter, his voice a soft drone of tenderness. When the baby quieted, he handed her back to Melanie.

"Well, I feel foolish," Melanie said, sniffling.

"Hey, I wanted to cry for her, too," he said, walking with Melanie to the front desk. "Navy SEALs don't cry—ruins the image."

"Ahh, my hero," she said.

He stilled, meeting her gaze, and sudden heat rippled between them. She'd said that to him once before when they were making love, and the memory of it flooded between them. Warm, wicked. Greedy. The softness in her green eyes said she remembered, too.

The nurse at the desk cleared her throat.

Jack dragged his gaze from Melanie. "I'm Juliana's father," he said to the nurse. "And her medical bills are insured by TriCare." He handed over a temporary card, his ID card, and Melanie frowned.

"What are you doing?" she said.

"She's legally my dependent, so she's entitled to the benefits. Though there aren't many anymore."

"I can manage this alone," Melanie said.

"I know you can," he said softly. "But it's there for her. I earned the right to have those benefits extend to her. When she's ten she'll have an ID card and use of facilities on the base."

Although they spoke softly, people were staring, listening. Melanie hitched the baby on her hip. "We can discuss this later."

"Sure," he said easily, taking his cards back and slipping them into his wallet. He walked to the far side of the room, opened the stroller and rolled it back to her. Juliana reached out for him, practically squirming to get to him.

Jack put her in the stroller, kneeling to strap her in. "You were so brave," he said to her. "I'm proud of you, princess." He dried her tears, kissed her head and with Melanie, led her out of the front door.

Almost like a real family.

Five

Melanie grabbed her handbag from her desk and was heading for her office door when her secretary popped her head in.

"Your one o'clock is here, Ms. Patterson."

Melanie glanced at the time, frowning. "They're very early."

"I tried to tell them that, but they seemed impatient."

Melanie shook off her disappointment of losing yet another chance to run home to see her baby. Besides, going home meant seeing Jack. Jack sitting on her sofa with Juliana asleep in his arms. Jack being a culinary genius in her kitchen and preparing some of the best meals she'd had in a year.

"It's all right. Show them in, Laura." She tucked her handbag in the drawer and moved from behind her desk, tugging at the hem of her jacket. Her welcoming smile drooped when the door swung open and Jack strode in with Juliana in his arms.

"What are you doing here?" Despite her protests, she went to him, taking her baby and hugging her close. "Oh, hello, sweetie," she murmured, and the baby giggled excitedly and squeezed her back.

"There is something to be said about a woman in a power suit," Jack remarked, standing close and letting his gaze roam leisurely over the deep-green designer outfit.

She met his gaze and suddenly felt beautiful.

"You've got the sexiest legs in this hemisphere."

She smiled. "And who has them in the Southern Hemisphere?"

He grinned and reached to unwind the baby's fingers from her earring. She always had a good comeback, he thought, and it was hard for her to take a compliment. "Don't know, don't care. How about taking a break with me?"

"I have an appointment who's likely waiting in the lobby."

"I'm the appointment."

Melanie blinked.

"I asked Laura to schedule some time, hoping that you'd go to lunch with us."

Us. It was enough to make her cave. Almost. Any time alone with Jack was dangerous to her heart.

"Jack, you can't take time from customers who need to see me."

"I opened an account for Juliana. So I guess that makes me a customer."

She felt cut off at the pass. "Why did you do that?"

"So I can start her college fund."

"I'm a banker, Jack. I've already started one. Before she was born, as a matter of fact."

"Ahh, but by then college is going to cost twice as much." His voice lowered and the deep tone coated her. "I helped make her, Melanie. I'm here to share the responsibility."

She couldn't protest that. It was for their baby, and she'd give up anything for her.

"So how about it?"

Melanie pressed her lips to her baby's head, missing her so much lately, then looked at Jack. The idea of sitting in a restaurant wasn't appealing.

"Come on." His smile was low-down sexy, and with the tight jeans, tight shirt showing off all that muscle, he worked magic on her.

Melanie wondered if she could stick to her resolve, because being near Jack was a cross between denial of what she'd like and danger of getting her heart broken.

At her continued silence, he arched a brow. "Scared to be alone with me still, Melanie?"

Her defenses rang out like a chime. "Lead the way, sailor." This was so she could spend time with Juliana. And if it wasn't for Jack being here, she wouldn't have had the chance, she reminded herself.

"Hmm, snappy attitude. I hear fear."

She rolled her eyes. "Give it up, Jack."

Not a chance, Jack thought and followed her out, his gaze dropping to her cute behind. He bit back a groan and the urge to drag her back inside the office and learn what color lingerie she wore underneath that green power suit. The idea was quickly drenched when half the staff rushed over to see the baby.

A few looked curiously at Jack, but he kept mysteriously silent as Melanie showed off their daughter. He had no idea what she'd told these people and he wasn't about to embarrass her, yet she inched closer to him and didn't seem to mind his hand at the small of her back. After she told her secretary that she'd be out for the next couple of hours, Jack urged her to the door.

An older woman stopped them, cooing at the baby. "I just have to say that your family is gorgeous."

"Thank you," Melanie said, looking at the baby. Juliana bounced in her arms.

"She has her father's eyes. You and your husband must be very proud."

Melanie's mouth opened to tell the woman he wasn't her husband, then she clamped it shut.

Jack stepped in and said, "We are. Thank you." He ushered Melanie out the door and to the car. Settling the baby in the car seat, they drove. Beside him, Melanie was quiet.

"Bothers you?" Jack asked. "What that woman said?"

"No, it's a logical comment. Juliana does look like you."

She was being evasive again, he thought. "Hair and eyes maybe, but she reminds me of you."

"I whine for my supper, too?"

Jack laughed. "She's stubborn, content with her surroundings and oblivious to what's going on right before her eyes."

Melanie looked down at her hands, flexing her fingers. "Then I'll be a six-month-old and continue to explore other possibilities."

"Liar. You're not even considering them."

"Jack, we've been over this."

His fingers gripped the steering wheel. "I never thought I'd have to beg a woman to marry me, but just give me one good reason why you won't."

"I'll give you more than one. You don't have to marry me to be a father—this past week proved that to me if it didn't to you. Marriage for the sake of giving a child her father's name is not necessary."

"It is if you're that kid."

She glanced at him, wondering about that stony look, then twisted in the seat to check on her daughter, who was happily chewing on a cracker and making a mess of Jack's car.

"I need more reasons than that."

"Jack, this isn't a 'Can you top this?' discussion."

"You made it that," he snapped as he pulled up beside a park He didn't say anything as he got out and went to the trunk. Melanie took her daughter from the car seat and just stood by as Jack became a master in baby-outing logistics. In less than two minutes he had a picnic spread under a tree far enough away from the other people enjoying the park to be private.

Melanie sat down and put Juliana on the blanket. Jack set out some toys, then opened the cooler and took out sodas. He offered one to Melanie and had his popped and half-empty before she'd taken a sip. She had the feeling that he wished it was a stronger drink.

"You're angry."

"Yes, dammit. You know, I've never proposed to a woman before. It's not something I'm going into blind."

He looked more hurt than angry and her heart split a little. He deserved to know it all. "Well, I've accepted proposals before and as a result, I've got my eyes wide open."

His gaze snapped to her. "You've been engaged? When?"

She felt his anger building and hurried to say, "Before I met you. One was a few months before."

Jack tried to keep calm, but the thought of Melanie agreeing to marry any man but him made him feel incredibly jealous and a little cheated. "What happened?"

Melanie took the sandwich he offered and with her other hand stroked Juliana's hair. "I loved Craig and he decided that his secretary was a better choice."

"How long were you engaged?"

"Long enough for me to be selecting china."

Jack groaned. "The guy was a moron."

"Yes, well, I take great comfort that his marriage to her didn't last as long as our engagement, but then about two years later I grew stupid again."

"Falling in love is not stupid."

"No, it's not. Marriage to the wrong person for the wrong reasons is."

Jack held his temper. Why did she think that just because they'd created a beautiful child before marriage they were so wrong for each other? "What did the second guy do?"

"You don't think it was me?"

"No, I don't, because you're a beautiful, smart woman, Melanie."

She held his gaze, wondering if he'd still be around if it wasn't for the baby they shared. She'd always wonder that, and it was a bigger reason not to marry him. "I found him in bed with a flashy blonde."

"Bastard."

"He said I was uptight and couldn't get with the program, whatever that meant. He was a professional football player."

Jack could hear the hurt in Melanie's voice even though she obviously tried to hide it. "Well, there you go. Cheerleaders, road trips, potential for mischief."

Her expressive eyes blazed like embers. "And that's a good reason to propose to me, then betray me?"

"No, it's not. There's no reason for that at all. But it wasn't your fault. The fault was in his character."

"Neither of them loved me enough not to stray, Jack. That's a mistake I won't make again."

She stared at her hands as she unwrapped the sandwich, and the pangs of sympathy and understanding swelled through Jack. She looked so lost and wounded. He clenched his fists against the urge to take her in his arms and ease the pain she was still feeling.

After a moment Melanie let out a breath and took a bite of her sandwich. "Oh, man, this is great. What's in it?"

"Something Emeril made on TV."

Her brows rose, her smile genuine. "You're turning into something I don't recognize."

"I haven't changed." His gaze fell on the baby. "Well, maybe a little."

"How's it been for you?"

"Scary. Wonderful. Proud. Scary."

"You said that twice."

"It's twice as frightening to know that I'm responsible for someone else's happiness. At least till she's eighteen, and by then I'll have her locked in a tower."

"Only knights in armor allowed?"

"Yeah," he said, grinning. "I think of what she'll look like in a few years, how she'll think of me."

"Yeah, me, too," Melanie said, and they both touched the baby at the same time. His fingers instantly wrapped around hers.

She met his gaze.

"Those other guys were fools. And I bet they're regretting the hell out of it right now."

"I doubt it."

"I'm not them, Melanie."

"Oh, Jack, I know that," she said softly, pulling free. "But if you and I got married, we'd be going in with more than roaming libidos against us."

"You're insulting me. I'd never do that stuff to you."

"You don't love me. That's the key here, Jack. I loved those men and was willing to overlook faults to be with them. So, don't tell me that a marriage will make things just magically work out. I've got the experience that says they won't."

"Other than the fact that those two men were not good enough for you, those were bad choices."

"And I'm not about to make another one by marrying for a name change."

"It's more than a name," Jack said, grinding his teeth. He wanted to tell her that he was a bastard, that he needed more than anything to give his daughter his name, but from Melanie's position that would not have made the can-you-top-this list.

But he knew now that she was protecting herself, her heart. He suddenly recalled the night they'd made their daughter.

Don't make promises you can't keep, she'd told him. *I'm not... I can't put my hopes on a man.*

She'd been jilted twice already and didn't trust her feelings enough to put faith in them. In believing there wasn't a chance for her and Jack beyond a name on a license, she couldn't get hurt again. It was bad enough she didn't trust him not to desert her, and even harder to deal with a woman who didn't think she had the potential to be worthy of a man's fidelity.

He wanted to pound those two men into dust for doing this to her.

But she was right in a couple of ways. He didn't love her. He was honest enough with himself to admit that. But what he felt for Melanie was more than just lust and memories of great sex. Even if Juliana wasn't between them, he'd have hunted Melanie down. He'd have done it to satisfy his ego that she hadn't forgotten him and to see if the dreams that had plagued him were just that—dreams. At the rate they were going, she wasn't going to give him the chance to find out.

And the baby changed everything. Better for him, for Juliana, but for Melanie and him, it had cut short what could have been something special, and Jack didn't know what to do anymore.

"Melanie?"

She looked up and the tears in her eyes were like gunshots to his heart.

"Honey, talk to me."

"I can't screw up your life for a name. Please don't ask me to. I know it would be better for Juliana, but you and I have to live with the decision and so does she."

He'd sworn he'd back off and this time he meant to keep the promise. He scooted close, his hand on the baby to keep Melanie near.

"I'm sorry you had it rough with those guys. But just don't forget that I'm not them." When Melanie opened her mouth, he pressed two fingers against her lips. "Shh. Don't say anymore. I can accept how you feel. I don't have to like it, but I can accept it. For now."

It was the "for now" that he clung to.

Melanie felt a little sprig of something wild inside her at the knowledge that he wasn't just giving up. Oh, she was sadistic, she thought, to have the perfect man in front of her and not want him. Well, that wasn't true. She did want him. She'd missed him terribly the past year, and now that he was here, she was pushing him away and not liking herself for it. But it was the never-knowing factor that helped her keep her distance. Never knowing if he could love her the way she'd dreamed of, of being cherished and needed, instead of a chain that locked him from his freedom.

Jack could almost see the thoughts churning in her bottle-green eyes. "We can be friends first. No strings."

Melanie arched a brow and looked pointedly at their daughter.

"Fine, a tiny one."

"Just consider me a full-time baby-sitter for the next few weeks, okay? Though you don't baby-sit your own kids, you raise them."

If anything he said could have won her over, could have let him deeper into her life, that was it.

"Friends, then." It sounded hollow and lackluster to her. But that's what you wanted, right? a voice in her head whispered.

An hour and half later, Jack stopped the car in front of the bank. Melanie glanced at her watch and sighed.

"You looked relaxed," he said.

"I am. Thank you, Jack. Lunch was wonderful."

He smiled, pushing back the urge to touch her.

Melanie looked into the back seat, smiling. "Well, she's wiped out."

He strained to see. Juliana's dress was rumpled and her knees were dirty from trying to crawl all over the park. "She's amazing."

He turned his head a fraction. Melanie's face was within an inch of his. And if he moved a fraction, their lips would meet. The temptation was eating him alive.

"Thank you for her, Melanie."

Her eyes glossed a bit. "You took part."

"Yeah, but I didn't carry her for nine months alone. I didn't suffer pain to get her here so I could love her."

He eased back a bit and gently brushed a strand of hair off Melanie's face. "Someday you'll tell me all about it? I hate that I've missed so much."

Missed so much of you, he thought. Of being the first one to know about the baby, of seeing Melanie grow round with their child and being there to hold her when she was scared.

"Yeah, someday." Someday, Melanie thought, she'd give him the video her father had taken during her pregnancy and the birth. The latter being something she wasn't ready to share with anyone just yet.

She turned away and opened the car door. He was there in an instant offering a hand. Her fingers slid easily into his and he tugged. "See you at home?" she asked.

His gaze raked her features. "Yeah. We'll be there."

He swore he wasn't going to do it, swore he'd back off, but he couldn't resist. She was taking his breath away by the second and he needed to touch her. Over the rim of the car door, he leaned and brushed his mouth over hers.

"Jack," she whispered, and there was no protest in her tone.

He didn't touch her anywhere else, just applied a bit of pressure, his lips sweeping gently over hers. Melanie made a tight little sound in the back of her throat, worrying his mouth, reveling in the taste of him. It was an aphrodisiac, a drug swimming through her system and making her want to be addicted to him. She could do that so easily. This, with Jack, was always good.

Gently he pulled back, his breathing a little faster, his eyes a little softer. A fractured smile curved his lips as if he'd just learned something he'd already known. He rubbed his thumb across her lower lip.

"See you later." He stepped back and moved to the driver's side.

Melanie couldn't move. Instead, she stared at him across the top of the car, then forced herself to turn and walk into the bank. Her steps were a little less steady and her pulse was…well, out of control.

Oh man, she thought, pushing through the revolving doors and ignoring the glances from her staff as she walked to her office. She went immediately inside, closed the door and dropped into her chair.

Oh man, oh man, oh man, she thought, pressing her forehead to the desk and letting out a long shaky breath.

They fell into a strange routine. Jack showed up in the morning early enough to have coffee with Melanie, and he was there when she came home at night. He cooked something fantastic every evening, and they dined together, but after Juliana was tucked in bed, he'd leave with a casual, "See ya."

Melanie found herself wishing he'd hang around a little bit longer, but she knew that would only lead to trouble. He hadn't tried kissing her again, but every time he was within a foot of her, she felt her insides clench and pull. She acted as if it didn't matter, as if she didn't feel it, but alone at night, she felt only the torment of need.

It was tough when she was learning so much about him and finding something else to admire. The veil between them was growing blurred and it didn't stop the feeling that she was being worn down. Therein lay the trouble, she thought. He was making himself indispensable. He'd be gone soon, off on some dangerous, classified mission that most of the government wouldn't know about, and that scared her.

It made her realize that with one mission Juliana could lose her father. And she'd lose a friend. Friends. Yeah, she thought. She never imagined they could come to that equitable of a relationship, but they had. Only, she was coming to expect him to be around, and his job said clearly he wouldn't be.

She was deep in those thoughts when she stepped into the house and called out. When she didn't get a response, she set down her briefcase and went looking for Jack. In the backyard, Juliana was in her playpen under a tree, and her father was building something fantastically large in Melanie's modest yard.

"Jack," Melanie said patiently, and he looked up. His gaze moved over her from head to foot and she realized he did that a lot.

"Hi, tough day?"

"Not as tough as yours, apparently." Melanie gestured to the pile of lumber and bolts. "She's six months old. She doesn't need a gym set like that."

"Every kid does. Besides, she'll grow into it." Jack kept working.

As she lifted the baby out of the playpen, Melanie's gaze slipped over the wooden gym set rising in her backyard. It hadn't been there this morning. He was getting sneaky, she thought. "You really have to stop this buying spree," she said.

"I didn't buy it. I made it." He tightened a bolt and stood, looking at her and not his work.

Melanie gaped at the castlelike set. "You made it? It's incredible, Jack. When did you have time to do this?"

"At night, at my sister's place."

"But you're here almost every night."

He shrugged big shoulders. "It's a simple design, and Lisa's husband, Brian, has a fair amount of tools in his garage. I did the cutting and sawing there. All I'm doing now is assembling it. The swing and glider were the hard stuff to find. Juliana and I just went on a search together during the day. The red swings were her choice."

Melanie smiled at him, hitching the baby onto her hip. "You are such a sap, you know that?"

He flushed a little. "Yeah. Besides, it's a father's right to dote on his daughter."

"But a stuffed pony?" She gestured to the taffy-colored stuffed creation as big as a real pony, resting near the playpen.

"Prelude to the real one I'll get her someday," he said just to get Melanie going.

Melanie smiled, shaking her head as she walked toward him. "You're hopeless. And no pony, ever. Unless you plan to clean up the mess and teach Juliana to ride. Because I have no idea."

"Me, neither."

"Fatherhood has destroyed your brain cells," she said, deadpan.

"Maybe we could all learn to ride together."

"I keep walking right into your verbal traps, don't I?"

"I'm not trying to trap you."

"No, you're not," she admitted. "Just wiggle."

He shot her a very manly offended look. "I do not wiggle."

She laughed and Jack felt knocked to his knees. She hadn't done that much while he was around. She kept her distance, emotionally and physically. And all he wanted to do was have both from her. He wondered how long he was going to last before the need to kiss her overtook him again.

He glanced at his watch. "You're home early."

"Banker hours." She smiled and stared at him. And there was a lot to stare at, too. He was sweaty and tanned, and the muscles in his shoulders and arms rippled as he tightened a bolt, then lifted the plank for the next piece. His tank shirt did nothing more than absorb the sweat pouring off him, and Melanie's insides clenched as she remembered what those damp muscles felt like beneath her palms. Beneath her mouth. Pressed against her naked flesh.

Oh, don't go there, she thought, and needed to put some distance between them. It didn't help that the memories of this man making love to her were just too vibrant to shut into a little corner of her mind.

"I'm going to change," she blurted, and he looked up, frowning as she rushed off.

Melanie hurried into the house, first changing her daughter's diaper and giving her a drink, then taking her into the bedroom while she changed out of her work clothes and into jean shorts and a light cotton T-shirt.

"Come on, sweetie, let's keep busy," she said, gathering up her daughter and heading into the kitchen. She put Juliana in her walker, then hunted in the fridge.

An hour later Jack stepped inside, inhaling the delicious aromas and running a rag over his face and the back of his neck. "You're cooking?"

"Don't look so surprised, Singer. I thought I'd give you a break, though I'm not quite the culinary artist you are."

He smiled, unreasonably touched. It was just a meal, but she looked adorable in the apron emblazoned with "Domestic Goddess" across the chest and with flour on her nose. He swiped at the flour.

"Mind if I use your shower?"

She went still for a second, just looking at him. "Of course not, go ahead." She paused in setting the table to fill a glass with water and ice. "Here. You need to replace all that water you've been sweating out."

He took the glass. "Thanks." He drained it without stopping, then let out a loud satisfied sigh.

Juliana copied him, beaming up at him.

Melanie laughed hard. "Good Lord, she's already picking up your habits," she said.

"At least they're not the really bad ones." Jack winked at the baby, then headed toward the bathroom, pleased that Melanie was more at ease around him. She'd been like an edgy cat that past few days. Ever since he'd kissed her outside the bank. He'd been more than tempted to try that again, but her avoidance told him that no matter the effect, she'd considered it a breach of trust.

He was drying off and pulling on his jeans when he realized his shirt was beyond hope. Going shirtless the rest of the evening was unacceptable. He'd have to go back to Lisa's for fresh clothes.

A knock sounded and he pulled open the bathroom door.

Melanie's breath snagged at the sight of his bare chest and damp hair. She held up a T-shirt. "It's yours. You must have left it here and it got tossed in with… It's clean. I thought since the other was dirty…well, here." She shoved it at him, irritated with herself that she was suddenly unable to speak around him. He took it. Smiling, he stepped into the hall.

She didn't turn away. She didn't move. It wasn't just the muscle and the sexy way he was looking at her, it was the man. In the past two weeks she'd learned more about Jack than she ever thought she could. And it was getting to her. He was getting to her. And the kiss they'd shared outside the bank was just a kiss, but it had made a lasting impression. A lingering one.

"I like it when you look at me like that," he murmured.

The sexy tone of his voice should have alerted her. "Like what?"

"Like you did in the elevator when you put my hand under your gown."

"I'm just giving you a shirt, Jack."

"Uh-huh." He took a step and loomed.

"For a man who deals in accurate details, you sure are reading more into this than there is."

"Am I?"

"Fine. Have it your way. Dinner's ready."

"Good. I'm starved," he said, staring at her mouth.

She could almost taste him, wanted to taste him, dammit. "Well, it's hot."

She started to move away, and he caught her, his hand sliding over her waist and wrapping her like warm silk. "Me, too."

Her hands went to his chest, her heartbeat tripping over itself. She could barely catch her breath. "This isn't wise."

"I can take only so much tiptoeing around you, Melanie." He didn't let her go.

She didn't push away. "I'm a big girl. You don't have to tiptoe."

"Darlin', I'm glad to hear that." He tilted his head and laid his mouth over hers.

The contact created combustion, and the flames licked around them both. Her arms slid up his chest and around his neck.

Melanie held on. And Jack fed the fire.

Six

He molded, he toyed, he played with her senses until she thought she'd scream with the sheer pleasure of it. Her body came alive, nerve endings suddenly raw and revved for his touch. There was nothing subtle in his kiss, nothing restrained. If Jack wanted to show her that in this, nothing had changed...he'd done so. In spades.

Need rocketed through her as he devoured, nipped, licked, his hand sliding down her spine and pulling her hips to his. The sharp contact sent a moan spiraling out of her, blooming vibrant and hot with the memory of how this man could wield enormous power over her desire. He owned it, and when his hand rode up her side to slide over her breast, she almost cried out with want.

Then Juliana did.

The sound ripped them apart, and just for a second Melanie stared up into his eyes, smoky with desire. She felt her insides give another small tremble, then she tore her gaze from his and went running on shaky legs toward her daughter. The baby stopped crying the instant she saw her mother, and Melanie sank into a chair, relieved. She struggled to catch her breath. Oh, she was a fine one to talk about restraint and being *friends*. Here she was making deals with Jack to be parents only, and she was falling into his arms at the sight of his bare chest.

Jack stepped into the kitchen, pulling on his T-shirt, then as if he didn't know what to do with his hands, he raked them through his short hair. Melanie knew he was there. He could sense her shoulders tightening an instant before she pushed out of the chair and went to the oven.

Jack moved up behind her, waiting until she'd lifted out the bubbling pan before he said, "I scare you, don't I?"

She hesitated, setting the pan on the stove, then let out a long-suffering sigh. "Yes."

"Why?"

"What do you want me to say, Jack? That I don't come apart at the seams when you so much as touch me? News flash, it just happened."

"I wasn't exactly a doormat, you know."

"God, do I," she said without thinking, and he laughed shortly.

"You turn me inside out."

She spun around sharply, meeting his gaze. "That's why we shouldn't be...you know." She waved the spatula toward the hallway.

"Trying to smother each other with our lips? Groping like teenagers?"

She reddened. "Well, that puts it in perspective."

He smiled, moving closer and loving the flare in her eyes. "Anyway you shake it, darlin', it's still there."

And so dangerous, she thought. If anything, those moments in the hallway reminded her that they were combustion waiting to happen and that she'd nearly forgotten her daughter in the face of her own need.

"I know. But sex isn't everything."

"It's a nice start."

Men, she thought, unable to stop her very supreme-female smile. They think first with their anatomy, then their hearts. "Okay, yes, I'll agree that in bed we were a great match. But is that all you want in a marriage? A name on a piece of paper and a partner in bed?" Melanie dished up the meal onto plates and brought them to the table.

When Juliana fussed, Jack set her in her high chair and gave her a cracker.

"No, it's not. But I think we have the makings of something stronger." Jack wanted to tell Melanie that she scared him worse than facing down enemy weapons with only one clip left in his magazine. He felt helpless around her and he wondered if she really knew what she did to him with just one of those innocent "oh, really" kind of looks she got when she was skeptical. That kiss already told her she had him roped and ready for her. And his body was still aching for more.

"Maybe." Melanie wasn't going to mention that because they'd had a child together, there was more

between them already and it also, very importantly
to her at least, masked true feelings. That fact tormented her because Jack was a good guy. She'd
found very little to dislike about him. What woman
wouldn't love a man who did the laundry and
cooked, for pity's sake?

Jack watched the emotions skate across her face
as he slid gingerly into a chair.

Melanie frowned slightly at him. "What's the matter? Are you sore?" He was shifting in the chair.

"Yes, I am."

"Want a heating pad, some ointment or something?"

He stabbed at a portion of meat, looking at her
through a lock of dark hair. "I don't think that is the
solution for this ache."

"Oh." His meaning sank into her like thick warm
honey as she sank into her chair. "Oh." And the
part of her that said, *Don't be so pleased, dearie,*
was lost to the sheer feminine joy of *He's hot for me
and still steaming,* which was shouting in the back
of her mind.

Melanie glanced up, her lips twitching.

"Eat," he commanded. "Or I'll come over there
and make you feel so good you won't be able to *not*
smile at me like that."

A giddy spurt of heat shot out to her fingertips.
"Aye, aye, sir. Viable threat noted. Shall I go to
Defcon Delta?"

Jack laughed, tossing down his fork and rubbing
his face. "It's Threat Con, not def. That's TV lingo."

"Oops." Melanie lost it and laughter bubbled up
from her like champagne.

It shattered the tension between them, and then they changed the subject and talked of everything but how they were sitting across from each other and wanting to share more than a meal.

An hour and a half later, Juliana was tucked in bed. Melanie gathered up toys as she made her way down the hall to the living room. Jack was on the sofa, the TV on and the volume turned low.

"I think I should get this on film," she said, and he looked up, a tiny T-shirt half-folded in his hands. "I doubt your teammates would believe it."

"I know they wouldn't." Jack continued to fold laundry. "These are interesting," he said, holding up a green silk thong.

Melanie leaned forward and snatched it from him. "Just fold it. No inspections." She tossed the panties into the laundry basket.

"I'd like to see those modeled. Or maybe these," he added, winging another pair of panties on his fingertip.

She took those away from him and went to the kitchen. "Go to the store. There are plastic females already dressed to model those."

He chuckled, then stacked the remaining clothes in the basket and pushed it aside. Melanie returned with a beer, handing it to him. He smiled his thanks and popped the cap. "I'm beat."

"Me, too."

"It's tough doing it all. I don't think half the men in the world realize what's going on in their own houses while they're away."

"Yeah, they have dreams of cleaning fairies and

a woman reclining on the sofa with a novel and bonbons.''

Jack made a face. "I don't think so."

"Haven't you ever heard of a man refer to his wife and say, 'I don't know what she does all day'?'' Jack nodded. "But then he doesn't consider who does the cleaning, the cooking, the raising of kids, school plays, teacher conferences and so on,'' Melanie said, sitting beside him on the sofa.

"Your mom do all that?'' Jack asked.

"Yes, and very well, I might add. She's my hero.''

Jack grinned and leaned back, the beer on his stomach.

Melanie shifted her shoulders in the cushions, staring at the TV. It was the Discovery channel and the words The Making Of The U.S. Navy SEALs flashed across the screen. She sat up, grabbing the control and raising the volume.

The commentator was explaining the training.

"Okay, this is boring,'' Jack said, reaching for the remote control.

"Not to me,'' she said, holding it out of his reach.

Jack groaned and sipped his beer. He didn't watch the screen. He knew what was happening and remembered his own training well enough not to want to relive it in color. So he watched Melanie, the way she bit her lip, the furrow of her brow. He wondered what seeing this show would do to the way she thought about him. He didn't think about being with the teams. It was like breathing to him now.

Melanie learned a lot in the first few minutes of the program. "Were you always Navy? The narrator said there were some guys that were Army, Marines, even Air Force.''

"I was a Marine first. I take a lot of ribbing for it," Jack said.

She blinked at him, then smiled. "Doesn't surprise me." She looked back at the screen and watched potential SEALs standing in the sea at night, linked arm in arm as waves hit them and instructors yelled. The men had been without sleep for three days. "That's cruel," Melanie said. "It's like torture."

"Nah, it makes the instructors see who can endure the worst and still want to be a SEAL."

"You did that?"

"Yes."

"Why would you put yourself through that?"

He shrugged negligently. "I wanted to be a SEAL. You have to do what it takes if you want something bad enough. Didn't you do all you could to be a banker?"

"No, actually I wanted to be a ballerina, but since I can't jump high enough, I changed my sights."

Jack laughed, shifting on the sofa lengthwise, wedging his feet under Melanie's hip. She didn't seem to mind.

"I've always been good with numbers. It doesn't mean I like it," she said.

"What would you like to do?"

"Something where I didn't have to leave Juliana with a sitter every day. Something I could do at home."

He didn't say it, but marrying him could give her that, and as if she sensed his thoughts, she ignored them and looked back at the TV.

"Are those real bullets they're shooting?"

"Yes, they're real. It's all real," he groused, and would have preferred she watch a craft show or something. "We can't train men if they know they're not experiencing real danger."

"What's it like when you're out there knowing you could get hit?"

"I don't think about it, Melanie. It's distracting." He worked his shoulders into the cushions, watching her and not the show.

And what kind of distraction would she and the baby be for him now? she wondered. "Are you afraid?"

"I'd be a fool if I wasn't. Fear keeps you sharp."

He still wanted to change the channel, but she refused, enthralled as she watched S.E.R.E.—Search Evasion Rescue Escape—training and saw several men drop out and ring the bell that signaled their final surrender.

Jack answered her questions, trying to minimize the danger involved, but Melanie wasn't fooled. The man sitting beside her had endured that training. He'd suffered crawling through mud, no sleep for days, eating food out of a trash can because that was all they'd been allowed the first days of training. Her admiration for Jack skyrocketed, and she tried to imagine him doing all that when she'd just seen him folding baby T-shirts and teasing her. It was like there were two men in him, and she admired the fact that both didn't show at the same time.

He leaves his work in the field, she thought, and wondered about the women who chose to marry men like SEALs and Marine Recon and Special Forces, who were the first ones in harm's way. Those women must live in fear for their husbands' lives the instant they walk out the door.

She was about to ask him about his buddies, but when she looked at him, he was asleep. She shut off the TV and moved to the edge of the sofa. Jack automatically stretched out his legs.

He'd look like a little boy if it wasn't for the muscles in his shoulder and arms that didn't relax. She stood, pulling an afghan over him.

His eyes flashed open and he started to sit up. "Sorry. Guess the sun today did me in."

Alert and ready to move, she thought. "More like a six-month-old girl, I think. No, stay there," she said, pushing him down into the cushions.

"You sure?"

"Yeah. It's late. Stay. See you in the morning."

Melanie locked up the house, smiling at him as she walked toward her bedroom and thinking she didn't have to worry about anyone breaking in, not when they had to get past a SEAL to do it.

The next morning Melanie's alarm went off as usual, but when she stepped into her daughter's room, she found the crib empty, and panic swept over her. Then she remembered Jack was here. Pulling on a robe, she walked into the living area and found him reading the paper and having coffee. Juliana was chasing cereal around the high-chair tray.

When the baby squealed, Jack lowered the paper. His gaze slid over Melanie like warm sheets on a cool morning, and Melanie tightened the sash of her robe.

If offer card is missing write to: Silhouette Reader Service, 3010 Walden Ave., P.O. Box 1867, Buffalo NY 14240-1867

NO POSTAGE
NECESSARY
IF MAILED
IN THE
UNITED STATES

BUSINESS REPLY MAIL
FIRST-CLASS MAIL   PERMIT NO. 717-003   BUFFALO, NY

POSTAGE WILL BE PAID BY ADDRESSEE

SILHOUETTE READER SERVICE
3010 WALDEN AVE
PO BOX 1867
BUFFALO NY 14240-9952

GET FREE BOOKS and a FREE GIFT WHEN YOU PLAY THE...

SLOT MACHINE GAME!

Just scratch off the silver box with a coin. Then check below to see the gifts you get!

YES! I have scratched off the silver box. Please send me the 2 free Silhouette Desire® books and gift for which I qualify. I understand I am under no obligation to purchase any books, as explained on the back of this card.

326 SDL DQLN

225 SDL DRNK
(S-D-10/02)

FIRST NAME	LAST NAME

ADDRESS

APT.#	CITY

STATE/ PROV.	ZIP/ POSTAL CODE

7	7	7	**Worth TWO FREE BOOKS plus a BONUS Mystery Gift!**
🍒	🍒	🍒	**Worth TWO FREE BOOKS!**
♣	♣	♣	**Worth ONE FREE BOOK!**
🔔	🔔	🔔	**TRY AGAIN!**

Visit us online at www.eHarlequin.com

DETACH AND MAIL CARD TODAY!

"Morning," he said, and his voice was like velvet.

"Hi. You're up early." It was a crime to look that good in the morning, she thought.

Jack inclined his head to Juliana. "She was having a conversation with the mobile. I figured I was better stimulation."

Melanie smiled, said hello to the baby, then went into the kitchen for coffee. She returned and slid into the opposite chair, nursing the cup and thinking of the dreams that had plagued her half the night. All about Jack. Jack in danger, Jack walking through her door, Jack sitting across the table like he was right now. Jack making himself indispensable.

"I really should be getting a shower." She started to rise.

"Relax. You have time. I've already fed Juliana."

She lowered herself back into the chair.

"Hungry?" he asked, folding the paper and setting it aside.

"No, I can't eat this early."

Jack logged that into his memory.

"How was the sofa?"

"Lonely."

"Jack."

He just grinned. It was good to be here in the morning, he thought, and wondered how Melanie managed to get ready for work, what with the baby and short a pair of hands. "Does Diana show up this early?"

"No, not till I'm ready to leave. Juliana doesn't take too well to my leaving her in the morning."

Jack arched a brow. "She seems fine now."

"Yes, well, she gets breakfast with Diana. Juliana's not a morning person…well—'' Melanie frowned at her daughter ''—not usually.''

''Something to be said about having two parents around, huh?''

Melanie made a face. ''Even if you were here all the time, you'd have to leave for work early, too.''

''I know. But I take about ten minutes to get ready.''

''Bully for the trained SEAL,'' she said, and he laughed.

''Drink more coffee,'' he said.

She had a second cup and played with her daughter for a little bit.

''I might as well go get ready for work,'' she finally said.

The idea wasn't at all appealing.

Jack noticed how reluctant Melanie was to leave, and he took the baby from her. She disappeared into her bedroom and thirty minutes later, almost to the second, she came out looking ready to battle the corporate world, in a dark-blue suit and a crisp high-collared white blouse.

All Jack could think of when she was dressed like that was that under it all she was wearing lace and silk. It drove him nuts to know it, and he whistled softly. ''Look at Mama, Jules.''

Melanie flushed a little as she gathered her handbag and briefcase, which were exactly where she'd left them yesterday. As if on cue, the baby whimpered, reaching for her mother. Jack noticed the expression on Melanie's face. Guilt. She held the baby for a little while, talked with her, then glancing at the time, finally handed her back to Jack. Jack soothed his daughter as Melanie stepped into her high-heeled shoes.

"I'll see you tonight," she said.

"Can you get away for lunch?" Jack asked.

"I won't know till I get to the office. I'll call."

"Try. I'm sure Jules would like to see her mother more than just for meals and baths."

Jack knew it was a cheap shot, but it was the truth.

"I have to work, Jack, and no, don't say that marriage will change that. I know it would. But I can't marry for financial reasons and you know it."

"You won't do it for a name, for more time or for yourself. What will it take?"

Already half out the door, she met his gaze. "Love, you idiot," she said, and closed the door.

Jack let out a breath. Love. He certainly liked Melanie, a lot, and he wanted her, but what did he know about loving a woman forever? His own reservations plagued him and he cuddled Juliana close, soothing away her whimpers. He spent the rest of the day trying to sort out his feelings for Melanie and wondering if he ever did love her and told her so, she would believe him or think that he was saying it just to get his name on a certificate for his child.

Seven

Melanie laughed, a deep-throated sound that wafted through her backyard. But Jack, sitting across from her on the blanket, didn't return it. Of course, the baby food dribbling down his face could have something to do with that, she thought.

"Well, when she doesn't want something, she doesn't," he said resolutely.

Still laughing, Melanie came up on her knees and with a cloth, wiped at the globs. "Just think if it had been an apple," she said, giggling.

"I'd be out cold." Jack watched her, enjoyed the moment of having her close, touching him. She'd kept at least two feet away from him at all times lately. Since he'd kissed her.

"Oh, tough guy."

"You smell great."

"You smell like strained peas."

"It's hard for you to take a compliment, isn't it."

"No, not really."

"You just don't trust men to tell you the truth."

"Well, there is that," she said, and started to sit back.

He grabbed her wrist, holding her there. "I'll always tell you the truth, Melanie. I swear on my honor I will."

Melanie stared into his cool blue eyes and saw only sincerity. "I think I believe you."

He grinned, then before she could back away, he kissed her, quick and deep, a warm play of lips and tongue that made her insides yank tight. She was breathless when she eased back and finished feeding the baby. Who, much to Jack's disappointment, ate the peas she'd just spat at him.

"She knows you're a pushover," Melanie said at his pained look.

"I wish you were," he muttered under his breath, and when she asked him what he'd said, he smiled. "How about you go out with me tonight?"

She blinked at him, stunned. She stammered a bit before saying, "But what about Juliana?"

"We get a sitter like normal parents. Diana will do it, I bet."

"I haven't had time with the baby, I'd rather—"

"Chicken."

"Excuse me?"

Lord, he loved that righteous look of hers. "You're afraid to be alone with me without Juliana as a buffer."

She looked appalled. "I am not."

"Good, then we'll go out." He whipped out his cell phone, dialed Diana's number and within minutes lined her up as a sitter. Shutting off the phone, he smiled. "Dinner and a movie okay?"

"All right, fine. I'll go." What could she say? He'd backed her into a corner of her own making.

"I hear fear again," he goaded.

She made a face at him just as the alarm on his watch sounded. He silenced it and said, "Time for you to go back to work."

Where had the hour gone? she thought. She kissed her baby and was about to kiss Jack, when she caught herself.

"Got to go," she rushed to say, and stood. Jack gathered up the baby and followed her into the house, then to the door.

"Diana will be here when you get home. I'll pick you up at seven."

Melanie didn't argue. She'd already learned that Jack was a determined man. She was losing every battle with him.

It was just plain weird to be this nervous, Melanie thought, checking her appearance in the mirror again. She wanted to look good. No, great, she amended, smoothing the line of her green tank dress. She hadn't worn this since before she was pregnant and was pleased it still looked good. The simple lines were overlaid with a layer of chiffon flecked with gold, dressing it up a bit. Then the doorbell rang and her heartbeat danced a fine tune that told her this night meant more than just Jack's getting his way.

When she came out of her room, Jack was talking

with Diana. Wearing a navy sports coat, khaki slacks and pale-blue shirt, he looked more like a college professor than a member of an elite commando team.

His gaze moved over her from head to toe and back up. "You look incredible."

"Thank you."

He smiled, hoping she believed him. "Ready?"

She glanced hesitantly at the baby and Diana.

"Oh, go on, we'll be fine," Diana said, nearly pushing Melanie toward the door.

After Melanie kissed the baby, Jack steered her outside to the car. A few minutes later they were pulling into the parking lot of a quaint restaurant on the waterfront.

"I forgot this place was here," she said after the waiter had seated them.

"I bet there's a lot of things you've forgotten since you had a baby."

She had her face in the menu, a defense tactic, he decided. He liked that she was nervous. His own heart was beating double time.

"I haven't forgotten anything, just lack the time."

He pushed down the menu. "Didn't you used to paint?" When she nodded, he added, "When was the last time you did that or went out with a girl-friend? Or soaked in a tub for an hour and painted your toenails or whatever it is that women do to look that great."

She blushed, unable to be defensive when he com-plimented her like that. "When I didn't have some-one else to think about," she said, and met his gaze over the menu. "Are you going to spend the evening showing me the error of my ways—or are we going to have dinner and be adults?''

Jack's smile was slow in coming and he sat back in his chair, ordered wine and nodded. The rest of the evening swept past them in a delightful blur. They talked of everything except marriage and their baby. They debated politics and she learned more about the Armed Forces and the restrictions it puts on the men and women who serve. He told her about his teammates, and of the few who were married, he mentioned their wives. He spoke quietly of an old mission, leaving out a great many details, she knew, but it was nice to have him confide in her at least that much. His face lit up when he talked about Lisa, his mother and late stepfather, but when it came to his real father, he changed the subject to woodworking. He wanted to show Melanie some of the things he'd made, but they were in storage, along with his tools. It made her see that other than his bachelor-officer's quarters he had on the base, he had no real home. It left her stinging inside, because he was a good man and deserved more than he had right now.

She told him how she'd handled her broken engagements, how hurt her parents had been that she'd been betrayed, then she scolded Jack for calling her father.

"He already likes you," she admitted. "Though when I was pregnant, he was ready to hunt you down."

Jack just smiled, unaffected. "With a gun I'll bet."

Melanie didn't respond to that, not wanting to ruin

the evening. "Whatever you said to him, he's keeping it secret. He won't tell Mom or me."

"Good. It's between us."

Melanie's look was wary, but Jack wouldn't give an inch.

"A guy thing," she said at last. "Okay. I won't pester."

"You wouldn't get it out of me, anyway. I'm trained to withstand pleading and tears."

Melanie laughed at his teasing, dined on incredible seafood and drank a little too much wine. When the meal was over, they decided to skip the movie and take a walk on the waterfront. The gnarled oaks were dripping with Spanish moss and lit with tiny lights, the wind warm and balmy as it rolled off the river.

Jack slung his jacket over his shoulder and strolled beside her, barely resisting the urge to wrap his arm around her and pull her close. She did things to him, made his palms sweat, made it hard to breathe sometimes when he was near her, and right now, she looked like a willowy fairy with her deep-red hair and the glitter of gold flecks on her dress. Suddenly she stopped, shaking a stone out of her high-heeled sandal, and he lent his arm, chuckling to himself when she continued their walk barefoot. She didn't let go, her arm looped through his until she paused at the rail. Melanie inhaled the salty air. The slosh of water against the wall below beat rhythmically.

"I had a good time."

"It isn't over yet."

She glanced his way. "It's late, and Diana is—"

"She's fine. So is Juliana." When she looked to

argue, he sighed. "And here I'd thought we were being adults and you'd relaxed."

Her brows knitted softly. "We are. I have. It's been wonderful. But—"

"Hush up, Mel."

"What?"

There was that look again, he thought. "You're going to talk yourself out of a good time if you say anything else." Jack stepped up to her, and without laying a hand on her, he kissed her.

Melanie didn't bother to deny herself the pleasure. Staring at this man across the dinner table, heck, all week long only fueled her need.

He kissed thickly, a slow torture of his incredible mouth, his hands clenched at his sides, and when she dropped her shoes and pressed herself against him, only then did he wrap her in his arms and hold on. Their kiss grew vibrant and steamy, yet held a tenderness they'd shared only once, moments before he left for his mission fifteen months ago. It was a small taste of the man he'd been back then, of the woman she'd been, and that the moment could be recaptured hadn't escaped either of them.

Jack eased back, drawing in needed air and pressing his forehead to hers. "Don't say anything."

"I wasn't going to."

"Yeah, sure."

"Except..." Her eyes teared a bit as she tipped her head back and swept her fingers up over his jaw, across his brow. "I missed you, Jack. I really did."

He groaned and held her, rubbing her spine, then whispering, "I hate that you had to be alone, Mel."

"I didn't miss you because of Juliana. I missed

the man I hadn't had the chance to know," she said, loving his arms around her, feeling safe and cherished.

Jack's throat tightened and he kissed her again, gently, with a tenderness that spoke of hidden emotion and not need.

It didn't scare her. The old feeling of distrust didn't rear its head and warn her off. Melanie just let herself feel, without thoughts of marriage and their baby and what the future might bring. Emotions flowed within the fraction of time suspended just for them. She touched his face, his lips, pushed at his hair.

He kissed the corner of her mouth, her cheek, sank his fingers into the auburn mass of curls spilling down her back. She was so incredibly beautiful and strong, and Jack knew there was more between them now, at this moment, than there had been since they'd shared a bed fifteen months ago. He brushed his mouth back and forth over hers softly, and when some teenagers on skateboards came flying around the curve of the stone walk, he scooped her out of their path.

"Reckless kids," he muttered, then asked, "Are you okay?"

"Yes, my hero, I am," she said, smiling.

Jack's gaze prowled her features and something inside him seemed to fill and fill, until the pressure in his chest ached. It left him stunned.

"Oh, dear, I think my shoe's a casualty, though."

Jack stared at her as she bent to pick up her maimed sandal. He took it, deemed it salvageable enough for the walk to the car, then bending to his knee, he slipped both shoes on her feet.

Melanie held his gaze, feeling the air charge with a current she couldn't name. Didn't want to examine. "Come on, Sir Galahad," she whispered. "Let's go home."

He stood, grasping her hand and tucking it in the curve of his elbow. "Galahad had pure thoughts, Melanie. I don't."

Laughing, they strolled toward home.

A few minutes later they stood on her porch, the door half-open.

"Do you want to come in for coffee?"

"No, if I come inside, I'll want more than coffee." His gaze raked her hotly. "And more than one kiss."

"I see. Then I guess a nightcap is out of the question, huh?"

"Yes, it is," he growled, backing her up against the doorjamb. "Because I can barely stand not having you, Melanie, but the next time I make love to you, I want my ring on your finger and vows between us."

Before she could speak, he kissed her hard, closing his arms around her and pulling her body flush against his so there was no doubt in her mind what he meant, what he wanted.

Then he let her go, spun about and climbed into his car. He drove away, leaving Melanie weak-kneed and wanting, and distrusting her own judgment.

Jack felt the change between them, the strength of the bond that went beyond the child, but he kept it to himself. Melanie was a strong woman, but trusting a man again scared the living daylights out of her. She deserved to be wary, and he still wanted to pulverize the men who'd hurt her.

He glanced at the woman pushing the stroller beside him in the park. Did she realize, as he had, that they'd fallen into a routine with each other? She might sleep alone every night, but she knew he was there. Just as he couldn't forget what it was like to wake up beside her, to feel her long legs and arms wrapping him.

"That's not the look of a proud father," she said softly from beside him.

He smiled at the flush in her cheeks. "No Galahad here," he murmured, adding a long velvety look over her body. It had become a joke between them, a message only they understood. He'd kiss her or touch her, she'd warn him off and he'd claim not to be Sir Galahad. Jack knew the only thing keeping them apart was her distrust. He was trying to earn her trust, though he hadn't given her any reason to distrust him. He was paying for some other man's crime, and while Jack wanted to bide his time, he was running out of it too quickly.

They'd circled the park and were heading back to Melanie's place when she paused near a bench to adjust the restraining strap of the stroller. An elderly woman sitting there was feeding the ducks that lingered near the small pond.

"Oh, aren't you a pretty little thing!" she said to Juliana, and leaned out to brush her fingers over the baby's hair.

Juliana gurgled and made bubbles for the woman.

"Thank you. We think so," Melanie said.

The woman looked up at Melanie. "She has your husband's eyes."

"Oh, we're not married," Melanie said without thinking, and instantly cursed her thoughtlessness.

The woman blinked, first glaring at them, then offering the child a look of pure pity that Melanie couldn't ignore.

"You poor dear," she cooed. "Raised a bastard because of selfish parents."

Jack stiffened and pulled the stroller well back from the old woman. "I see that being inexcusably crass has nothing to do with age," he snapped.

Melanie looked between him and her child, fighting the welling of tears.

The woman sniffed, then huffed out an indignant breath. "Well, it's your own fault, you know. I won't be the first—or the last to say it, either, young man. You ought to be thinking of this innocent child and not yourselves. Since you weren't thinking of her when you made her."

Melanie gasped, then grabbed the stroller and wheeled it away. Jack clenched his fists at his side and being an officer and a gentleman, refrained from telling the woman exactly what he thought of her.

He went after Melanie.

"Don't say anything," Melanie muttered without stopping.

"Melanie, honey, stop."

"Damn that old bat." On her front steps, Melanie burst into tears. "How could she say that to my baby!"

Jack swept his arms around her. "Shh." He pressed his lips to the top of her head and Melanie sobbed. Juliana chimed in. "Come on." He ushered his women into the house.

Once inside, Melanie sat on the sofa and cuddled the baby. Juliana continued to whimper.

"Melanie, hon, you're scaring Juliana."

"I know, I know. Help me, please." She handed the child to him and went to wash her face. In the bathroom she sobbed with helpless anger, and when she came back, he'd put the baby in her crib.

Melanie went to go check on her, but Jack stopped her. "She's fine."

She scowled. "Let me go."

"You're upset and she knows it. Come on, relax a little."

"I don't want to relax. I want to stay mad."

"Good, then let's talk about this." He urged her toward the sofa.

"We've done that." She plopped into the cushions.

"Have I asked you to marry me again? Have I reminded you that we should do this for her and not us?"

Melanie felt battered by her own words and feelings. "No," she admitted, "you haven't." She snatched up a pillow and plucked at the edges when she wanted to punch that old woman. "But nothing has really changed, has it? We're not going to see marriage in the same way. You see names on paper and I see lifetimes."

Jack felt her words sink into him like arrows. "What do you want, Melanie?" When she remained silent, he took the pillow and forced her to look at him. "What do you want?"

"I want a marriage like my parents have, where what they do, they do together. And not just for the kids, but for themselves, because they loved each other first." She swallowed hard. "I want to be loved because I'm me, Jack, not because I'm Juliana's mother."

"But you are her mother, and that's not going to change."

A leaded feeling coated her heart just then. "And she's the reason you're still here."

His features darkened. "Not true."

"And how would I ever know that for certain?"

"You won't. You just have to trust me."

She scoffed and pulled free. Jack felt helpless, watching her close the door again and secret away the key just when he'd managed to find the lock.

"I think your being around is just making this harder on both of us, Jack."

"Maybe you're right."

She looked up, still as glass. His gaze locked with hers for a moment, then he stood and headed to the door.

She rose and rounded the back of the couch. "Where are you going?"

At the door he stopped, his hand on the knob, his gaze clinging there. "I don't know." He looked at her, wanting a magic wand to make things perfect and realizing they never would be. "All I know right now is that I want you in my life like there will be no tomorrow. I care about you and I love my daughter. I'm sorry it's not enough. I was just trying to make things right for our baby."

"Jack."

"I'll see you later." He stepped out and closed the door.

Melanie stared at the door, a knot working up her throat as she sank slowly into the nearest chair, stunned. What have I done? she thought. What now?

Outside the door Jack stopped, wanting badly to turn around and walk back inside. To take Melanie into his arms and kiss her until she couldn't argue with him anymore. He left the porch and climbed into his car, driving toward his sister's place. Every mile he put between him and Melanie didn't help. But she did have a point. She was the mother of his child and nothing would change that. And Jack had to ask himself if that was all he wanted from Melanie. Their names on a license? What did it mean, in the long run, to marry her for the sake of a name? To keep old women like the one in the park quiet? He pulled into Lisa's driveway and shut off the engine, sighing back into the seat. When had he thought of marriage as just names? When had it come down to that between him and Melanie? Jack knew why he wanted his daughter to have his name, but was he ready to tell Melanie?

He slammed out of the sports car, marching to the door and throwing it open. Inside it was dark, and the loneliness that he'd lived with for years screamed back at him. He'd handled it with a fair amount of ease in the past, but the thought of getting a call that would take him away right now made his stomach clench. He didn't have a normal job. He didn't have normal hours, for that matter. It was get a call and go do the job. Up until now he hadn't been afraid of dying, either. Now he was. Because Juliana needed him. Melanie didn't. She'd proved she could handle anything on her own. It also meant that when he had to leave, she could handle it all. He snorted to himself. Yeah, you act like you matter, he thought.

If they married, she'd be a Navy wife, and she'd also have a ring on her finger that would keep her from finding someone she could truly love. Oh, God, he thought, dropping his head back against the closed door. The idea gouged his heart. Deeply. Was he asking too much of Melanie to sacrifice her chances for his need to give his daughter his name?

It was actually comforting to know that nothing would stop Jack from being with his daughter. But then, loyalty was one of Jack's better qualities. He came around when she wasn't home and left before she arrived. The completed play set in the backyard wasn't the only reminder that he'd been in the house. He did the laundry, cooked and then, like a magical partner disappeared. Diana had no problem telling her how wonderful Jack was to the baby, but that, too, Melanie didn't have to hear secondhand. It showed in Juliana, the way she looked around for him.

And Melanie missed him, craved to look into his eyes, to see him here where she could share with him. Oh, hell, she thought. She needed him, she wanted him, and while she struggled with her feelings, it wasn't until she took her daughter to the doctor for a follow-up appointment that Melanie got another cruel taste of what Jack had been arguing about for the past weeks.

"You're single?" a nurse, new to the clinic, asked as Melanie settled the bill.

"Yes."

The nurse glanced at the baby, then at Melanie. "And the father's name?"

"Lieutenant Jack Singer. It's all right there in Juliana's record."

"You're not married to the father, so how can she have military TriCare benefits?"

"You'll have to ask *him* that." All Melanie knew was that Jack had arranged it, had been looking out for his daughter the only way she'd allowed him to.

"Illegitimate status might cause a problem, since the child isn't listed on his service records."

Illegitimate.

It rang as harshly as *bastard*. Melanie felt her insides tense and she gripped her daughter a little tighter. "Fine, put the visit on mine." She handed over her own insurance card.

"Yes, ma'am." The nurse gave her a testy look, then quite plainly snubbed her child.

Melanie snatched her card back and without waiting for a receipt, she left. Yet for the first time she felt the stares. Not so much on her, but on her child. An innocent baby who had nothing to do with the marital status of her parents. Damn, Melanie thought as she drove home. Damn those people. If it was this bad now, how bad would it be when Juliana was in school? When other kids picked up things from their parents and called Juliana names? By the time Melanie arrived home, she was on the verge of tears. Juliana fussed, sensing her mother's turmoil. Melanie gave her a bottle and changed her for her nap, but she couldn't help thinking of what it would be like years down the line. When kids would talk. When people would be cruel.

The decision came easily.

Eight

The knocking was frantic, and when Jack opened the door he didn't expect to see Melanie. In tears. "My God, Melanie, what—"

"I'll marry you."

"What?"

"I said I'll marry you. Right now. Today, tomorrow." She pushed her way inside and he closed the door.

"Wait a second. What's going on? Is Juliana all right?"

Melanie swiped at her cheeks and nodded. "She's fine. She's with Diana."

Thank God. His heart slipped back from his throat to his chest. "Now sit down and tell me what happened."

"I got another taste of someone just like that old woman in the park."

"I see."

"And it hurt." She clutched her throat, choking on her tears. "Oh, God, it hurt and I wanted to hit something."

"I know what you mean."

She looked at him. "I've been selfish. I didn't see how my single status could affect Juliana, and the last thing I want is to let anyone hurt my child."

Melanie fell apart again, filled with guilt and anger, and Jack came to her, closing her in his arms. She gripped him and cried.

"It was awful. They looked at her like she was to blame. She's just a baby!" Melanie moaned low in her throat. "I'm so ashamed of myself."

"Shh," he said. "It's all right."

"It's not all right, dammit. It's unfair."

"We'll make it right, for her, not for us."

Was it all really for the baby? Melanie wondered. Was that all Jack wanted? His name after their baby's on a birth certificate? "It's what you've been saying all along."

Her tone was so disheartening Jack asked, "Is marrying me so bad?"

She lifted her face to his. Her gaze slid over his features as she thought of all he'd done, of the man he was. Melanie knew she'd already started the fall into love the instant he walked back into her life. She'd tried to ignore it, but it kept coming. He kept coming. It wasn't just that he was a great help or that Juliana adored him, but that he was so willing to do right by both of them. All three of them. Melanie knew his honor was at stake, his feelings for their child laying the path. But what about his feelings for her? She understood all too clearly that he wanted her in his bed, but in his life? *Really* in his life?

It would change so much for both of them, but Melanie couldn't see the future. She didn't want to anticipate failure. In the past fifteen months she'd tried to be practical. She'd tried to do what was best for herself and her baby. And what she'd really done since he'd come home was protect herself and fail her child.

Juliana needed her father.

Melanie needed to be loved by him.

Because she was already falling deeply in love with Jack. Was she willing to risk her heart being broken again? Then she thought of her daughter, that one ugly look from the nurse that Melanie would have done anything to shield from Juliana.

"What are you thinking?" he whispered softly. "I can see those gears grinding in your head."

Her lips curved gently. "No, you can't."

"You're trying to talk yourself out of marrying me."

"No, I'm trying to figure out why you would want to give up your freedom for us."

"I love Juliana."

"Of that I have no doubt. But what about you and me, Jack?"

He sighed. "You know how I feel about you."

"I know how your libido does, but what about you?"

Jack struggled with his words, with whether or not she was ready to hear what he had to say. And whether he understood it himself. He'd spent half the night trying to gather his feelings into a neat package and failed. "I...I don't know."

She stiffened.

"Can you say the same thing?" He felt his breath snag in his lungs.

"No, I can't. My feelings are jumbled and Lord knows I've tried to piece them together since you came back." She pushed out of his arms and dug in her purse for a tissue, then tossed the handbag on a chair. "I care about you a great deal, Jack." Well, that was cautious, she thought. "And I know it's not because of Juliana, since we've been living without you for a while." She looked at him. "But you haven't. You came into a ready-made family."

"Yeah, so?"

"Come on, it's not that easy."

"No, it wasn't. It was a shock. But all I had to do was take one look at my little girl and I was lost. And her mother still does crazy things to me."

"I'll never know if you care for me because of her or for myself."

"You'll have to trust my word."

She couldn't quite bring herself to do that. Not yet. And if he shouted to the heavens that he loved her, she wouldn't believe him, anyway. There was still a huge part of her that didn't trust a man to tell the truth and mean it. She'd thought the other men in her past were decent men, good men, up until they betrayed her. Or was she just not seeing them for what they were at the time? Was she blinded by her love? Granted, they hadn't been in a tough situation like the one she and Jack were in now, and the gloves were off with her and Jack. There were no claims of undying love to sway her.

Oh, but she remembered her heartbreak when she'd learned the truth about each of her fiancés. Keeping herself at arm's length wasn't a bad thing, but Jack wouldn't stand for that. Despite his desire to commit himself to her and their child, was he ready for what Melanie wanted from him?

When she remained silent, staring at him with that odd look in her eyes, Jack's heart folded over itself. "You have good reason not to trust men, honey. But I haven't done the things those others have. I'm not leaving and I'm not looking elsewhere, either."

"And if you did find someone else?" Saying it out loud stung her.

"I don't want anyone else."

"Because I'm the mother of your child."

"No, because you're the woman I want."

Melanie felt as if an arrow landed right in her heart. For a moment right then, she believed him. She smiled.

He returned it, then his expression sobered. "I will never betray you, Melanie. Never."

She stared, wanting to trust his words. Wanting to just *believe* him.

"You'll let me know when you trust me, right?" he said, and she blinked.

How could the man read her like that? It was irritating and a little comforting. "Yes, I will." At least he'd accepted the fact that right now, she was borderline.

Jack took several measured steps toward her, watching her eyes flare as he approached. He grabbed her close and kissed her, leaving nothing hidden, nothing undone. And she came apart in his arms, her fingers driving into his hair, her body meshed with his and yielding for him.

"Marry me, Melanie."

"Yes," she breathed.

"Just so you know," he said against her mouth, "I plan to be a husband in every way."

Her heart skipped to her throat. "Oh, goody."

He laughed and kissed her again, and his hands found their way beneath her blouse, to her skin. She flinched with the sweet contact. She could barely stand when he touched her, and he dropped into a padded chair, pulling her onto his lap.

He spent several minutes working his magic on her, and when her hand slid down to the bulge in his jeans, Jack groaned and set her on her feet.

She blinked, breathing hard.

He strained as he stood. "I need to call someone."

"Excuse me?"

He smiled patiently and cupped her face in his palms. "I told you, baby, when I made love to you again there would be vows between us."

She slid her hands up his chest, smoothing her thumbs over his nipples and listening to his breath hiss out through his teeth. "Get a move on it, sailor."

Two days later, with Lisa at her side, Melanie promised herself to Lt. Jack Singer. He'd managed miracles for this moment. The small chapel was filled with flowers, a couple of his teammates were sitting in the pews, and her parents, much to her surprise, were there. While Melanie's mother sobbed quietly,

Jack's mother sat with Lisa's husband, Brian, all three grinning foolishly. Beside Jack, SEAL team leader Lt. Commander Reese Logan stood as Jack's best man, not showing a shred of emotion. It made Melanie see the differences between Jack and his teammates. They were reclusive and almost cold, especially Reese. But Jack, she thought, was an entirely different man. And right now, he couldn't stop smiling.

In dress whites, he listened to the chaplain, but his eyes were on her. She felt them coat her like warm syrup, touch her in places she didn't know still had life. And when Jack said "I do" and slid the most incredible ring on her finger, Melanie struggled to breathe. Then she gaped at the diamonds.

"This is forever," he whispered. "All of this." And at the chaplain's command, he kissed her.

Married.

Melanie expected her head to scream *What have you done?* yet her heart was shouting *Oh, yes* as Jack dipped her back and kissed her like a lusty groom.

They parted, smiling at each other until his teammates muscled their way between them to slap Jack on the back and offer congratulations. Melanie hugged her parents, yet her gaze stayed on Jack. Despite the small crowd around him, he was also looking at her, and she felt cherished and desired. It made her heart stumble, yet she didn't have time to think as his teammates converged on her. It had to be illegal to have so many good-looking men in one place, she thought, as a SEAL hugged her.

Jack stood back as his teammates kissed his wife,

glaring at the youngest member who took full liberty and a little too long in letting Melanie go.

Reese was at his side. "She's beautiful, Jack."

"Yeah, I know."

"Does she know what she's getting into being married to one of the teams?"

Jack frowned, then smiled. "She married me, Reese, not the SEALs."

"You know what I'm talking about."

"Yes, I do. And Melanie's been doing fine on her own, so she can handle military life." Jack glanced at his buddy. "Is that why you've never taken the plunge? Because you don't think there's a woman out there who can handle the need-to-know factor?"

"It has its drawbacks," was all Reese would say.

Jack knew there was more behind that statement, but he wasn't going to pry right now.

"Well, not every service member is single, Reese. Think about it," Jack said, then headed toward his wife.

Wife.

It stopped him in his tracks, and he was filled with waves of pride and something else he wasn't ready to name. Melanie was leaning down to comfort her mother, who couldn't seem to stop crying with happiness. Jack's gaze slid over his bride, her lush body wrapped in a slim-fitting satin gown of the palest lavender. While the top portion was a simple tank style with thin beaded straps, the skirt hit the floor and fishtailed in the back. It was the sexiest wedding dress he'd ever seen, and it showed off her curves to maximum effect. All he wanted to do was push everyone aside and explore each of those curves.

Being in a chapel and surrounded by friends quashed that idea, and he moved up beside her, wrapping his arm around her.

Melanie stiffened for a second, unaccustomed to him touching her so freely after keeping him mostly at arm's length for the past weeks. As if he sensed it, he rubbed her spine and pressed a kiss to her temple.

"Come on, let's feed these people, get them all drunk and slip away."

She tipped her head to look at him, her lips twitching. "Sir Galahad, you've planned for everything."

He grinned. "Just looking out for every contingency." She smiled and he whispered for her ears alone, "You look more beautiful than I've ever seen you, Mel."

"I feel that way." She touched the side of his face, ignoring the camera flashes and the people around them. "Thank you for all this."

His gaze raked her ruthlessly. "I won't let you down."

"I know."

The two words were the start of the trust Jack needed, and he kissed her gently.

But it wasn't him she was worried about, she thought as they left the chapel and headed to the officers' club. What if she let him down?

Melanie sipped champagne and stared out over the wide river. She was amazingly content. Though this was the first time she'd been parted from her child overnight, her parents were having fun with their grandchild, and Jack's mother was planning to join them in the morning for an outing. Yet with the knowledge that she wasn't alone anymore, the anxiety she'd carried for some time slipped off her in waves with each passing moment. Somewhere behind her in the suite, Jack was tipping the bellman for room service. She'd known he'd go all out. The ceremony spoke for itself, and she didn't question how he managed to get all those people together so quickly. That was Jack. He made things happen. She smiled to herself and took another sip of champagne. The slap of water against the seawall seemed to match the occasional glitter and pulse of the stars in the blanket of night. She pulled the combs from her hair and shook it out, tossing the combs aside and letting the warm breeze sweep over her.

She felt Jack come up behind her, her senses tuning into him like radar. She leaned on the balcony rail. "I'd forgotten how beautiful it was in this town."

"For the first time since I arrived you look peaceful."

She glanced at him as he moved up beside her, his uniform jacket already discarded somewhere in the suite. The white T-shirt stretched tight over his muscles.

"I am." She stared at her goblet for a moment, then looked out over the moonlit water. The trees sighed with the breeze, Spanish moss dancing like a lacy hem beneath a skirt of branches.

"I'm a little relieved, too."

"How so?" He sipped his drink, then put it aside, resting his forearms on the rail and folding his hands—mostly to keep them off her when he wanted badly to touch her.

"I didn't really want to be a single mom, Jack."

His brows shot up.

"I thought I did. But when you showed up and bullied your way into my house—" he smiled at that "—I realized how much Juliana was missing. How much my life was a bit—" she shrugged "—empty."

Her confession fueled the idea that she'd done this for more than their daughter. "It looked pretty busy to me," Jack said.

Melanie ran her finger around the rim of the goblet. "I want you to know that if you find someone else and want out, I'll understand."

"I won't."

"Excuse me?"

He grinned, took the glass from her and, setting it aside, drew her into his arms. "I thought I was keeping you from finding someone else, too, but I don't want you looking elsewhere."

She wouldn't. She knew that in her heart that very second. "Demands already?"

"I have what I want," he murmured, his gaze lowering to her mouth. "Can you say you're satisfied?"

She threw her arms around his neck. "Ask me in the morning."

His smile grew wider by the second. "That's what I love about you, Melanie—you never say what I expect."

"What are you expecting? And if you say nothing, I'll know you're fibbing."

He met her gaze steadily. "Fidelity, honesty and your trust."

Both realized he didn't say love, yet neither acknowledged it.

"Two out of three?"

He settled his arms more comfortably around her. "I know you trust me. You just don't want to admit it."

Cocky, isn't he, she thought. "How would you know?"

"You wouldn't have married me if you didn't trust me a little. And I know you wouldn't have let me get this close to you again, either," he said, and laid his mouth over hers.

Melanie felt something inside her unwind, go loose and languid, then wrap around him. Ribbons of desire slid along her body with every second he kissed her. It was slow and tender at first. He molded and toyed, nipped and licked, playful and patient, and when she thought she couldn't draw in air fast enough, he moved to her throat. He kissed the base of her throat, slid his tongue lower, and she felt the sudden exquisite rush he gave her splinter over her. Her arms slipped from his neck and she palmed his chest, wanting his hold to tighten, to be stronger. Because she'd been alone for so long. Because she'd missed this man. Only this man. It was like finding safety and contentment in his arms, as if it had been stripped from her when he left that day, and only now was she allowed to let the feelings back into her heart.

His touch weakened her and she loved it. The strap

slid off her shoulder, and her zipper was slowly undone, the snug bodice easing from her.

"It's been eating at me all night."

"Oh, yeah, what's that?" She tipped her head back as his mouth made a damp path over the swells of her breasts.

"Wondering what you've got under this gown."

"Not much."

He groaned. "Every time I saw you go to work, I knew there was something completely feminine underneath your business suits."

She laughed. "Is that so?"

"Yeah, my imagination would be a good weapon of torture." Jack leaned back, anticipation rocketing through him and making his fingers ache. The bodice gaped and Melanie wiggled. The satin fabric whispered down her body to her ankles.

Jack swallowed. "My imagination didn't come close."

She smiled, lifting the gown from the balcony floor and tossing it onto a lounge chair. There was something decadent about being on a balcony in nothing but her lingerie, she thought.

And even more decadent with Jack eating her alive with his eyes.

"Man, oh man." His hand coasted up her side, over her iridescent lavender stockings, the thin strap of her thong. Her breasts were cupped in the sheerest fabric edged in lace. He met her gaze. "I'm done for."

"Liar, you never give up. And is that any way for a SEAL to behave?" she said, tugging his T-shirt from his trousers and backing him into the room. She peeled his shirt off over his head, flinging it aside with a smile too seductive for words.

Jack's mouth went dry. He'd wanted her for so long, had wanted her nightly for a year and a half. The last person he'd made love to was Melanie. The last person she'd touched like this was him. And until he died she would be the only woman he would love. Jack stilled and looked into her eyes.

Her brows knitted ever so slightly, her gaze probing. Suddenly he cupped her face in his palms and kissed her, long and leisurely. Melanie felt it, the tender mercy of it, the electricity they'd always shared tempered with something new.

"Jack."

"You're mine, Melanie. Mine."

There was something in the way he said those words, something so possessive, so certain that it left her shaking. Then she realized he was trembling a little.

"I want you," he said. "All night, all day, forever."

Melanie swallowed thickly, feeling confused and cherished and needed all in the same breath. She could feel his heart beat, hear his erratic breathing that matched her own and knew this moment had changed something in him.

Jack reached to pull her close, but she batted his hands aside and tugged at his belt buckle. Her smile was feline wicked and her gaze never left his as she opened the buckle slowly, kissing his mouth, his throat, bending a bit to lave his nipple. The air hissed out of him between clenched teeth.

Then her hand dipped inside his trousers, closing

over him. He growled, his fingertips digging into her waist, his body aching for her in every cell, every pore.

Melanie watched the play of emotions skip over his features, felt his shuddering breath vibrate down to the floor. His hands were busy, drawing her against him, forcing her to release him and hold on. He cupped her breast and she moaned in response, touching him everywhere. He bent and hooked a finger in the cup of her bra, pulling the sheer fabric down. Her nipple spilled into the heat of his mouth, and he bent her back over his arm. He suckled warmly, his touch growing stronger, then easing, stronger, then delicate.

It drove her wild and she plowed her fingers into his hair, crying out, holding him close. "Oh, Jack."

He cupped her buttocks, pulling her against his heat, then his fingers slipped beneath the band of the thong, following the line of it curving her hip and lower, then pushing it aside. He slipped a finger between her legs and she gasped over and over.

He absorbed each sound, his groin tightening. She mewed softly and he kept stroking her as he laid her on the bed, hovering over her.

Melanie felt everything in her yank and twist, the pulse hot and quick with lush desire. "Oh, Jack, not yet."

"Look at me," he growled, and she did. "We're just starting. Don't you remember, baby? We were never done when I had to leave last time." His motions quickened and he watched her eyes flare, her body erupt with her climax. Her muscles flexed and clawed and a little shriek escaped her as she bowed back, rocked against his hand and took her pleasure. She cried out his name again and again, and it made him smile.

He kissed her gently and she sank into the bed boneless. "Catch your breath fast, baby. I mean to have more of you."

She managed to lift her head off the bed and look at him, but he was already in command. He hooked her panties and pulled them off, mapping the contours of her legs with his lips and teeth, gently nipping at her calf, her thigh and higher. He rolled the stockings down, tasting each inch of flesh revealed, then with her leg propped on his shoulder, he stripped off his trousers.

Melanie let her gaze lower over him as he kicked the white slacks aside. He was a wall of muscle, a warrior, his waist lean, his abs rippled with definition. Just to look at him made her body quiver with want. To touch, to taste.

Jack watched her look and felt himself harden to near painful proportions. She was open to him, bare and uninhibited. She had no fears, only need in her green eyes, and when she clapped her legs around his waist and drew him down, he wanted only to give her pleasure, to make her as delirious as she was making him.

His arousal brushed her center and she arched, the move hungry with demand. But he didn't give her what she craved, and laid a moist path over her mouth, her cheek, down her throat.

"I want you now," she moaned.

"Did I ever tell you that in training we have to stand in the water for twelve hours in the dark?" he said casually, then his lips closed over her nipple and he drew it deeply into his mouth.

"No. Ahh, Jack."

"I love it when you say my name like that." He tasted her other nipple, feeling her writhe with each pass of his tongue. "We learned patience." He slid lower, taking his time tasting her soft, smooth skin. "No food, no water, but we can see it. It's on the shore. It makes the need worse. To see it, smell it and not be able to have it. So your patience has to be greater than your need."

"Yeah, I...oh, yes..."

He kissed her belly, then slid lower. Running his hands under her spine, down her buttocks, the backs of her thighs, he nipped and licked, his mouth circling her abdomen, yet never touching where she craved. "The feast is in plain sight and we can't have it."

"Uh-huh." She knew she should be paying attention, but it was useless. Her thoughts were swimming in pleasure, her nerves and body tingling with anticipation. His mouth passed over her skin, leaving a burning trail of want, for more, much more. She could scarcely breathe. And why was he even talking?

He smiled, knowing she wasn't listening and wondering how he could get the words out when his need to feel her body trap his had his blood pounding like an engine. Her fingers balled in the bedspread, and her hips rose in invitation.

"Well." The heat of his words breezed over her liquid center. "I was never very good at it," he said, then tasted her.

She came unglued for him. It was what he adored about her. She never held back. He laved and stroked her, his movements languid and succulent. She gasped his name over and over, told him how good she felt, that she wanted him inside her, and her erotic words nearly undid him.

He pushed her thigh farther over his shoulder and drove deeper, letting her come to the edge of rapture, then slowing and taking her up the peak again.

"Jack," she screamed, and he rose up.

She labored for air, wrapping her limbs around him. "Now, Jack, please."

"Yes," he said softly. "Now."

He lifted her farther onto the bed and shifted between her thighs. Braced above her, he met her gaze.

Melanie went still, her nerve endings exposed. Her heart exposed. She'd wanted this for so long, and gazing up at him, she reached between them and closed her fingers around his arousal.

Then she let the silken tip of him slide against her.

"Melanie, honey."

She smiled like a cat and guided him. He sank into her slowly and she watched his muscles tighten, his head drop back for a second or two. His entire body flexed as he pushed and filled her completely.

"Mine," she said, and moved, her hip retreating. He plunged. "Don't you forget it." Her voice cracked and she pushed harder against him, demanding, claiming.

He met her tempo, a smooth cadence heightening their pleasure with each stroke. Jack felt it climb up his spine, shatter his will. She touched his face, kissed his mouth, his chin. Jack grabbed the headboard, leveling himself, watching her as he left and plunged into her body. She stretched beneath him, long and willowy, utterly feminine in her passion. He was aware of her every nuance, every movement and sound she made. Yet it was the tears in her eyes that snagged his soul and tore through his heart.

He called her name, his chest vised with tenderness. Desire slapped at them like waves, splashing over them. The slick folds of her gripped him, drew him back.

Pleasure, it beat. *Love is here,* it whispered.

Soft and womanly, she yielded to his strength, his power.

Bronze captured in a delicate pearl, he was her prisoner.

Their passion was like a living thing, curling around them, simmering on the edge of their skin. It throbbed from one to the other, twisting until they were more one being, than simply two joined. He held her gaze, never breaking eye contact, never ceasing his movements.

Then he lowered onto her.

"I need you," she whispered, and her voice caught. "I need you for more than this, Jack."

His throat thickened, and he knew what she couldn't say. He felt it. In his bones. Then exquisite heat rolled up his body, into her and exploded. It blinded him with its power, and he thrust hard. She cried out, bowing like a silken ribbon beneath him, and he pushed and pushed, shoving her higher on the bed as their climax dragged them over the edge of rapture, and kept on dragging. It razored through him and into her, ripping out on a soft groan.

Desire suspended between them, a silent thread of a moment. Fused to her, Jack buried his face in the curve of her shoulder and held on tightly. Passion wouldn't let him go.

When it began to fade, when he thought there would be nothing left of him but ashes, Jack knew his heart had left him somewhere, and he prayed it landed inside hers.

Nine

He smoothed her hair back from her face and kissed her deeply, with as much fervor as before, with a devouring hunger that lent itself to the side of demand.

She responded instantly. She didn't have a choice; he owned her desire. Possessed her when she hadn't thought she wanted to be possessed so strongly. But she did, she was, and when he rolled to his back, taking her with him, Melanie lay draped over him and sighing with satisfaction.

They didn't speak, still catching their breaths, yet he palmed her spine, her buttocks, in a slow roam. She lifted her head, then folded her arms on his chest, propping her chin there. His expression was serene, his eyes closed.

She wanted to tell him what she was feeling, but

she just wasn't sure. And she wasn't ready to commit her heart so deeply, though she already knew she'd taken a tumble when Jack walked back into her life. Now he was in her bed again, making her feel much more than before, and she wanted him to know how much of a woman she was with him, but she decided that he already knew. He was the only man who could make her rip apart with her desire and still want more.

He opened his eyes. "Hi."

She smiled. "Hi yourself, Lieutenant."

He squeezed her buttocks. "I'm almost afraid to hear what you have to say."

"I'm not talking myself out of anything, Jack." She inched up, running her tongue over the seam of his mouth before she kissed him.

He groaned, trapping her in his arms.

"We're amazing together, aren't we?" she said, and he shifted them to the side, running his hand over the curve of her hip.

"Oh, yeah."

"So what happened when you stayed in the water for hours?"

He cocked a look at her, amused. "I didn't think you were listening."

"I wasn't, but that much I caught."

"We finally got to come in and we ate the leftovers from the previous meal out of the trash can."

"Eww," she said, sitting up. "That's disgusting."

"All a matter of survival, darlin'. You're hungry, you eat what's there." From his position, her bare breast was too much of a temptation. He tipped his head and took her nipple deep into his mouth.

Her sharp indrawn breath filled the room, followed by a low throaty moan. Melanie knew she was moaning. It was hard not to be vocal when Jack touched her like this. He cupped her breasts, kneading them as he sucked, the pull sending spirals of sweet sensation out to her fingertips.

Her toes curled.

Only him, she thought, scrubbing her hands over his chest and then lower. The muscles of his stomach flinched and she smiled to herself. He nuzzled between her breasts and Melanie shifted lower, leaving hot grinding kisses in her wake. His breathing labored, his grip on her tightened.

"Melanie."

She met his gaze, stroking his stomach, her hand gliding over his skin, then slowly closing her fingers around his arousal. He was already hard. She arched a brow.

He just shrugged and grinned. "It's a perpetual state with you around."

Then she bent and licked. He howled and she took him.

"Oh!"

Jack was helpless. Sinking fast and furiously into the sensations rushing and churning inside him. His body reeled in ten directions at once. His hands fisted in the sheets. His blood shimmered in his veins and rushed to collect where she touched. She tasted. He couldn't stand it. He *wanted* to stand it, but he was almost embarrassingly powerless.

He grasped her under her arms and pulled her upward. "We better do something about that," he growled. "Now."

"Thought I was." Melanie smiled as she straddled his hips. He didn't give her a second to breathe, pushing into her and bucking. She laughed and spread her hands over his chest, riding him, rocking hard and watching his face. He rose up, pulling her legs around him, then quickening their motion. Gazes met and locked as their bodies beat a frantic rhythm.

Sweat trickled, damp flesh melted. She gripped his shoulders as he pushed and pushed.

"You are so hot," he said against her mouth. And she told him what he did to her, what he felt like inside her, thick and pulsing. It fueled him and he tossed her on her back and thrust harder, faster, and she laughed and begged for more. He sent her across the bed and they fell to the floor, never stopping. Groping, pushing, filling.

Then the shock came. Like a savage beast, their climaxes roared through them, pulses pounding. Blood boiling and spilling back into their hearts.

"Melanie," he chanted over and over as they fused, smiling as his body poured into hers. He shuddered hard and she trembled with the power of it. He went slack, sapped of energy, and he sank onto her for a second, then knowing his weight was crushing her, shifted to his side.

"Hoo-yah," he groaned into the bend of her throat.

She laughed between gasps for breath. "Go Navy."

He burst into laughter, then kissed her into another mindless puddle of desire.

Eventually they made it back into the bed.

*   *   *

Jack belted his robe, running his fingers through his damp hair and staring down at Melanie. On her stomach, a pillow tucked close, the sheet draped her behind and nothing else. His gaze moved over her long hair, down her slender spine. The legs that had trapped him to her last night. He smiled and shook his head, amazed and pleased. Hell, more than pleased. But then, he'd known it would be like that. Tender, wild and all over the place.

Beyond the windows the sun rose over the river, and he took the cordless phone and moved out onto the balcony where he'd set up their room-service table. He smiled. He'd refused to let the bellman inside. He wanted no interruptions, nothing to disturb these moments alone. Reality would show itself soon enough.

His gaze on her, he dialed her house, waiting for her mother to answer. Melanie would be anxious to know how Juliana fared without her. He was not anxious to know how either of his women would fare without him. But his time was growing short, his leave was almost over. His country, he knew, would soon call.

Melanie sat up sharply, confused, and when she realized she didn't have a baby to care for, she sank back into the bed. She stretched, taking a refreshing breath, and realized she was alone. Quickly she scanned the room and found Jack. Her heart did a little leap and she tossed the covers aside. He was already sitting on the balcony, reading the paper and sipping coffee, and when she walked near, he looked up and smiled.

"Now that's a pleasant sight in the morning."

She smiled and reached for her robe.

"Damn."

"I don't think the town is ready for nudist dining."

He smiled and she sat beside him. He poured her a cup of coffee, and she tipped her head back, enjoying the warmth of the morning sun.

"What shall we do today?"

"I need to call Mom."

"Already done. The princess is, as we speak, being whisked away to the park, then the beach and then shopping."

Melanie smiled, trying to not miss her child and to focus on Jack. "Did you have something in mind to do today?"

He gave her a velvety look.

"Besides that." Last night they'd played and explored and discovered. And Melanie thought, he's not running off to some mission. I can still get him near for a while.

"Sailing, a tour?" He hesitated. "Shopping?"

She laughed. He looked utterly horrified at the possibility. "I wouldn't dream of forcing you to shop. Besides, I really don't need anything."

"Considering your gender, that's a first."

She nudged him. "Chauvinist."

Jack smiled, and his heart did a little lurch when she brushed her hair back and the sun glittered off the diamonds on her hand. The last time he'd made love to her, he'd slipped out in the early morning and headed to Asia. He never forgot about her. Too many times to count he recalled being on ship in his bunk and wondering what she was doing, if she'd forgotten about him. She was in his blood.

Now she was his wife. She wore his ring and he wore hers. He looked down at the ring she'd placed on his finger during the ceremony, the simple band of gold meaning more to him than he thought possible. Forever, he thought, and met her gaze. She was watching him.

"You can't wear that on missions, can you?"

"No. No identifying marks. Does that bother you?"

"No, I wouldn't want you to get hurt because of a ring and I don't believe a ring makes you married. It's more than that." She sipped her coffee, breaking off a piece of a muffin and popping it into her mouth.

"Keep going."

She glanced at him, then looked out over the water. "It's commitment, compassion, honesty. Trust. Those things are marked with a ceremony and a ring, but they don't make them happen. I learned that the hard way."

He caught her chin, pressing his lips to hers, then pulling back enough to say, "School's over, baby."

Her eyes teared and she touched the side of his face, falling into his kiss. "I know." Her voice wavered. "I really know that." She searched his features and Jack saw her uncertainty, saw the fears.

"Talk to me."

"I don't want to let you down, Jack. You've done so much."

He tipped her face up. "Hey, this isn't about who does more, Melanie. I'm getting all the benefits—a wife, a daughter…a friend."

"You haven't mentioned lover."

He smiled.

"Kiss me again, Lieutenant."

"Yes, ma'am."

Boy, did he. Melanie felt her insides yank tight the instant his mouth touched hers.

"I'll want to do that forever," he whispered against her mouth and pulled her onto his lap.

Melanie sank into him. Forever. It was the same for her. She knew she wouldn't have agreed to marriage if she wasn't sure there was more than sex and a baby between them. She couldn't admit to herself that she loved him. Not yet. Trust was coming, but her heart had tricked her badly before. She would have sworn she loved her fiancés, but this was so different. Jack was different, strong, patient, powerful.

Did she have to choose badly twice before she chose wisely? she wondered when Jack's hand worked inside her robe and her train of thought disintegrated. He palmed her breast, whispering how soft she was, how he loved just holding her.

"You're more than holding, Singer, and you best stop or get busy," she teased, and he grinned and his hand shot downward between her thighs. He nudged them apart and pushed two fingers inside her.

She choked.

"Busy enough?"

"Oh, yeah," she moaned, curling toward him as he stroked her to incredible passion. Her hips rocked and Jack stood, carrying her into the bedroom and setting her on the bed.

Melanie was on fire and she tore at her sash and

flung her robe open. "Hurry," she said. "Right now, Jack."

He tore off his robe, his arousal full and throbbing. "Aye, aye, ma'am," he growled. Lowering himself and spreading her thighs, he pushed into her.

"Oh, Jack." She dragged his name out, long and soulful, as he plunged and plunged, cupping her buttocks and lifting her to greet him.

There was nothing gentle in their lovemaking, only a frantic passion that overtook them in seconds. They clawed and dug at each other as they met and parted. Bodies didn't sheathe, they captured. Kisses were deep and hard and devouring. The crest rose with each thrust, and when Jack thought he'd hurt her, she'd demand more. He gave it, wanting this pleasure only with her. It was never typical, each touch seemed to be fresh and new and yet familiar. He plunged maddeningly deep and she locked her legs around him as they reached the summit and grabbed for more.

The explosion ripped a cry from her. Jack bit his lip to keep from screaming like a fool as pleasure erupted in savage demand. His legs and arms trembled as shudder after shudder razored through his body.

And when it subsided, when they were limp and sated, Melanie laughed.

He lifted his head to stare down at her. "You laugh? Laugh when I can barely breathe?"

"No, I laughed because I remembered why I went to the hotel room with you in the first place."

"My charm?"

"I knew it would be mind-blowing exciting."

He rolled off her and lay on his back. "I'll take that as a compliment."

"Don't. Your ego is large enough." She stood and he watched her cross the room to the bath, his gaze on her behind. A second later he heard the shower running.

"Hey, Singer," she called. "You waiting for an invitation or what?"

Air. He was waiting for breathing to come easily again, he thought, smiling as he pushed off the bed, crossed the room, then pushed open the door. Through the clear glass he saw her in the shower, wet and soapy. All she did was arch a brow and run that sponge over her breasts, and he was ready for her again.

He stepped under the spray and murmured, "You're going to kill me, woman." Then pushed her up against the tile wall and loved her again.

Melanie stared out the window into her backyard, watching her father inspect Jack's handiwork on the castle-style gym he'd built for Juliana. The two men hit it off famously, sharing some secret bond. Her father had told her already that he thought Jack was more than a good choice for her, but he didn't elaborate on what the "more than" meant. She wondered how shocked her father would be that she and her new husband had been romping all over the place, buck naked till the wee hours.

Smiling privately, she watched Jack and her father inspect a joist. Jack's father, David, had passed away two years ago, which was the reason Jack had escorted his little sister down the aisle at her wedding, but she learned that David had been a wonderful, calm man. She suspected Jack got that from him.

"You don't know what to do with yourself, do you, honey," her mother said, and Melanie glanced back over her shoulder. Jack's mother and hers were sharing Juliana like a great prize. The baby was in Grandma heaven.

"Both of you are going to spoil Juliana so badly I'll be tearing my hair out when you're not here."

"Grandmas' privilege," Laura, Jack's mother, said. "We get to have all the fun and none of the work." With that, Laura handed Juliana a biscuit. "Do you have any chocolate?" she teased.

Melanie laughed and, shaking her head, went into the kitchen. Jack's mother was great, a cut-up like Lisa. It was all…perfect. Perfection in anything but numbers on a bank account scared Melanie. And it was strange. Strange having Jack in her house, his things in the bathroom. She wasn't territorial or anything and had made room for him. But she had to smile when they awoke in her very feminine bedroom. He looked a little silly there. But that was the only place. Waking up beside him, staring across the dinner table, talking late at night, it was all so real and comforting. And it had only been a few days. While Jack learned she gave great back rubs, she realized he could repair just about anything. Juliana loved that her daddy was near, and though Melanie had some time off, she almost dreaded going back to work. And dreaded the moment when Jack would leave for duty.

Laura came into the kitchen carrying snack trays

and dishes from their barbecue. Melanie reached for them.

"I got it." Laura started rinsing and loading them into the dishwasher. "So how you doing, honey?"

"Just fine. Great, actually."

Laura, who was petite with dark hair that showed very little gray, moved a little closer. "You sound shocked."

She looked at Laura. "I wasn't expecting for it to be this…easy."

"It wasn't easy getting to this spot though, was it?"

Melanie scoffed to herself. "No, ma'am."

"I knew there was something between you two at Lisa's wedding." At Melanie's glance, Laura wiggled her brows. Melanie laughed and knew where Jack got his charm. "I just didn't know how much, and when Jack called to tell me he was a daddy, I knew it was you."

Melanie's brows shot upward. She and Laura had spent time together during Lisa's wedding, and though she lived out of state, most of the preparations had been taken care of by Lisa and Melanie. And Jack, when he'd arrived. "I'm glad you approve, Laura."

Laura patted her hand, her voice low and private. "I understand what you're going through. Sometimes it works and it scares us. We're waiting for the other shoe to drop, the roof to fall." Laura was staring out at nothing, a sweet private smile on her face. "Then sometimes you just get more than a little lucky."

Melanie prepared a pot of coffee. "Jack's a good man. We're married and we're friends."

Laura laughed sharply. "Friends? The way the two of you look at each other?" She leaned close. "And buddies share a bed, right? Pals can't keep their hands off each other, although we all know you two have to try real hard. I hate to see the two of you the minute we all leave."

Melanie blushed ten shades of red.

Laura laughed again. "I've seen the way Jack looks at you. He's drunk with loving you."

Melanie's gaze snapped to Laura's as she poured detergent in the dishwasher. "Oh, I don't think so."

Laura folded her arms and smiled as she leaned back against the counter. "I know my son. I know his reasons behind wanting to marry you, and the two of you may talk a good game, but I can see it in his eyes. He can do that Navy SEAL thing, looking all cool and aloof, but it doesn't hold up when he looks at you. So you keep telling yourself this is just for my granddaughter's sake if that helps you accept it. But I know better."

Melanie almost resented that.

As if Laura sensed it, she stepped close. "He loves you. Madly."

Melanie closed the dishwasher, her hands shaking as she switched it on. Laura slipped out of the kitchen as Melanie looked out the windows at Jack. Love her? He'd already said he couldn't give her that. Melanie wondered what kind of fool she was even to consider the romantic ideas of his mother. Laura wanted them to be happy and in love, but that didn't make it so. Marriage didn't automatically mean happily ever after, especially when they married for reasons other than love.

And what if he did love her? Could she trust it? After all, Craig and Andy had said the same thing, and look what happened. Jack hasn't said so, either, she reminded herself. But she also admitted that everything she had with Jack was different. Very different. She'd never felt the electric charge go through her with one look until Jack. Never wanted to be with a man twenty-four/seven until Jack.

As if her addiction was trying to prove her right, she moved to catch a glimpse of him. The men were having a beer and discussing woodworking, she didn't doubt. God, Jack was handsome. The black polo shirt combined with the black hair made him look dangerous. Desirable.

Laura strolled past, laughing to herself. As if to say, "See? Told you so."

Jack wanted her in his bed, wanted to be near his daughter and to have his last name on Juliana's birth certificate. Which he'd had changed the day they'd returned from their honeymoon. He had what he'd wanted. Would he leave now? Melanie wasn't going to fool herself and live in a dreamworld, believing he loved her. Just thinking about it would drive her insane, she thought.

Why? Because she wanted his love?

How was she ever to know? she asked herself again. He was kind, considerate, and there wasn't much about him she didn't like.

Adore. You adore him, a voice in her head shouted.

Yes, she did. She was falling into love with Jack and it was easy. So easy. But there was a little part of her that refused to accept it. As if she'd be tricked and lied to again.

Ten

Jack frowned down at the wrapped box tied with ribbon. There was no mistaking that it was for him, since the card stated his name. He called out for Melanie, tossing his keys on the table.

She walked out from the hallway. "Shh, she's sleeping."

"What's this?"

"What's it look like?"

"A present for me, but why?"

"Open it and find out, silly."

He eyed her, his lips curving slightly. He tore open the package and lifted out the heavy toolbox. "Man, this is a nice one."

"Look inside."

Setting it down, he flipped the heavy latches. It was filled with tools: tape measure, level, a hammer, screwdrivers, even a power drill and handsaw.

"You said all your tools were in storage, so I thought you might like to have a set here."

He lifted out the drill, checking it out the way only a man could, she thought. Boy toys.

"Thank you."

She frowned. "You don't seem pleased."

"I am, I love it. It's very thoughtful, but..." He hesitated and her heart sank a little.

"But?"

"I'll have my things with us. When you and Juliana come with me to Virginia. I won't be stationed in this area. There are no teams here."

"Well, that I knew."

"Now you don't sound pleased."

"I've tried not to think about it just yet." Truth be told, Melanie didn't want Jack to leave. Their relationship was growing stronger by the day and she wanted it to have a better chance before he left.

"You didn't think I was just going to return to work and drop back in when I have leave, did you?"

She smiled now. "That, Lieutenant Singer, I never considered."

He set the tools aside. "Are you prepared to move?"

"Prepared mentally? No." She tipped her head, holding his gaze. "Is that necessary right now? You're gone a lot."

His lips quirked. "Ready to kick me out?"

"No," she said without hesitation. "Of course not, but I can handle being alone."

"Oh, I've no doubt about that. I had to muscle my way in."

Her smile was small and a little embarrassed. "You don't have that problem now, do you, sailor?"

He moved close, settling his hands on her waist. "I'm stationed where they tell me to go, and right now it's Virginia. It's nice there, and there are other Navy wives you could meet."

"I'd like to meet your friends' wives. I would."

"You're not ready to commit that far, huh?" He lowered his hands.

"No, it's not that. I'm up to the challenge and we're in this marriage together," she said, pulling him back to her. Melanie didn't like the hurt way he'd looked at her, and she couldn't just do this half-heartedly, not being married to a man who risked his life every time he went to work. "Sure, I'm willing to move, too. We're husband and wife. In fact, it would be an adventure," she said, warming to the idea. "New town, new community. Fresh start. Changing locations would certainly make Juliana a more well-rounded person."

"And sometimes she'd lose the friends she'd made. So would you."

"I'm a big girl and you act like I haven't thought about this, Jack. I have." She sighed and looked at her hands, spread over his chest. "I just don't want to be afraid for you."

That touched him and stung in the same instant. "I'm good at what I do."

"I know."

"Hey." He tipped her chin up, moved beyond words that she was worried about him. "Let's not think about that right now. How about we start planning? You can look up some real estate on the Internet, learn about the area. Because I don't want my wife and child that far away from me. I'll go nuts.''

Any arguments Melanie had faded quickly with the look in his eyes. "You mean that, don't you?"

"Hell, yes. The thought of leaving you in a couple weeks scares the heck out of me."

Him? Scared? "Why?"

"Because I'm just now getting you to believe in me, and I feel like if I disappear, we're going to backslide." It was his greatest fear, that all they had would be destroyed because he had to leave soon. He didn't like this uncertainty when he was certain they should be together. He wanted to prove to Melanie that she had his heart, and he was fast running out of ways to convince her that he wasn't going to break hers.

"That's not going to happen." She found it odd that she was convincing him now.

His gaze raked her. "You so sure?"

"One thing I know right now, right this minute, Jack, is that what I feel for you is more than I expected and just what I wanted."

He grinned. But her features were somber. "Just don't lie to me. I don't think I could stand it," she said.

A horrible guilt passed over his spine. He still hadn't told her he was a bastard, the real reason he'd insisted on marriage. And right now, the words wouldn't move past his lips. He told himself it didn't matter, but the tiny voice in his head said he'd better tell her all or she'd never forgive him. And tell soon.

Melanie followed the notes Jack had left. It was cute, she thought. She took the glass of wine from the fridge and sipped as she made her way to the bathroom as instructed. The note said he had Juliana with him, and he was picking up Chinese food after a quick visit to the grocery store.

She followed his instructions and stepped into the bathroom. Her breath caught, and something sharp touched her deep in her heart. Steam rose from a bathtub filled with bubbles, and though only two candles were lit, several circled the tub. It smelled like lavender and rosemary, and the rough day she'd had, which she'd complained about, melted away with the anticipation of soaking in the bath. She set the glass aside long enough to tie up her hair and strip off her clothes. The water was near scalding hot and her muscles relaxed. She sank to her chin and closed her eyes.

This, she thought, was pure heaven.

Jack set the bags of Chinese food down on the table, Juliana asleep in his arms. Quietly he changed the baby and put her down for the night, glad he'd bathed her earlier and feeling terrible for forcing the child to stay awake while he shopped. But he had plans with her mama.

He laid Juliana in her crib, tucking her in and bending to kiss her. The child smiled in her dreams and it cut his heart in half and made it spill with hard emotions. She has me in her fist, he thought, closing the door. The baby monitor was on, and he tucked the receiver into his back pocket. He knew where Melanie was, and as he headed to the living room, he heard the sound of water in the bathroom. Temptation clubbed him and he paused at the door, pushing it open a crack.

Her hair was piled on her crown, and a mountain of frothy bubbles surrounded her shoulders. The lights were off and each candle was lit, flickering around her. Steam rose from the surface. Her eyes were closed.

"You're letting in a draft," she whispered.

"Do you know what you do to me looking like that?"

Her eyes flashed open and across the short distance he felt electrified.

She smiled. "I have an idea. This was very sweet of you, Jack." She reached for her wineglass, sipping. "It's just what I needed."

"After the bad day you were having and whining about, I figured some downtime would make you sleep better."

"All you had in mind was sleep, huh?"

He gave her an innocent look. "Of course."

"Liar. Wanna get naked and wet with me?"

He smiled, stepping inside and leaving the baby monitor on the sink. He stripped and she watched him, loving the jump and flex of his muscles. Hottest body on the planet, she thought, delighted that he was hers. She shifted and he slid into the tub. Water rose to the rim. She was glad she'd opted for the garden-style tub when she'd bought the house, she thought, although she'd never had a man in her tub. She'd never had a man this deep in her life, she realized.

She offered him a sip of wine, but he shook his head, sinking back and just staring at her. She slid her foot up his leg, the water and slick oils in the bath making her dainty foot feel like silk passing over his skin. Jack felt himself grow harder, and when her foot slid higher, he caught it.

"Are you inviting me to play?" His look was dark and sly.

Her smile was devilish. "Talk is cheap, sailor."

He leaned forward, his big shoulders glistening with water, slick with bath oil as he slid his hands up her thighs, across her belly to cup her breasts. She let out a telltale moan.

His touch was a force to be reckoned with, addicting. She'd wanted him from the moment she got off work, wanted to feel his arms and his kiss and be soothed by his strength. Then he went and touched her heart by drawing a bath for her. How lucky could one woman get? And when he stepped through the door and looked at her as if he was going to eat her alive, she was helpless. With Jack she never had much resistance, and when his lips came into play, his tongue sliding luxuriously over her nipple before his mouth latched on, passion coiled around her in heat and steam and man.

"You know, there is some of my training that comes in handy sometimes."

"Oh, really? What's that?" she said, her voice a little slurred as his thumbs slickly circled her nipples, deeper with each stroke. She couldn't think of a thing beyond the stamina the man possessed, which would be beneficial right now.

"I can hold my breath for nearly two minutes."

"Really?"

A second later he was under the water tasting her,

and Melanie shrieked. "Oh, my goodness, my goodness!" she said, as pleasure slathered over her in hot thick waves. He gripped her hips, refusing to let her move as he tortured her, her mind struck between amazement and the erotic pleasure ricocheting through her body. Her heartbeat was like a sledgehammer in her chest. Her legs went numb and trembled, her breathing wouldn't catch up with her need, and she grabbed at the side of the tub as he played her like an instrument.

Her body was singing to him; Jack was so in tune with her that he could tell when she was near, when she liked something. This she liked and he tormented her for a while longer, until he was certain she was struggling to hold back her climax.

"Jack...*Jack!*"

He straightened, smiling, raking his wet hair back off his face.

Instantly she climbed onto his lap. "Come here. I'm...I'm going to—"

"Yeah, I know. Mission accomplished, then," he growled, pushing into her, filling her in one stroke. She groaned deep in the back of her throat, grabbing onto his slick shoulders and thrusting. Her mouth mashed over his, her tongue spearing between his lips, and he felt devoured. She rocked and her pleasure made him harder, pulled him nearer to satisfaction. Her uninhibited desire pushed water to the trim of the tub, extinguishing candles. Slick muscles clamped him and she trapped his face in her palms as her climax spread through her like molten fire. The sight of it made him come unhinged, and he bucked, thrusting deeper and deeper, and feeling her body claw his in a velvet fist. Squeezing, flexing. Seething.

She leaned back, bowing, and his fingertips dug into her hips as convulsions beat a wild song through them. She fell onto him, her lips molding over his hungrily as her pleasure and his floated away on soft waves.

Jack let out a long breath, his hands smoothing her back as he laid back in the tub. Occasionally he cupped water and poured it over her spine.

"I am a contented man."

"Oh, yeah. Can I join the club?"

"Are you content, Melanie?"

"Yes." She snuggled in his arms, hating that the water was cooling so quickly.

"I know this is going to sound really stupid, but is it the sex?"

She snickered and leaned up to look at him. "You're kidding, right?"

Once she got a close look at his expression, her smile fell. "Oh, darling," she said, cupping his face and staring deeply into his eyes. "No, it's not. It's a plus, but if that's all it was, would I be so unhappy about you leaving for who knows how long?" Her eyes teared. "I'm your wife, Jack. For better or worse, I am. With you here or not, I'm still your wife." The words spilled from her, but she was too scared to speak right now of the feelings locked deep inside. "I want that. I cherish that. If the Navy says move here, I'll be with you. We'll be with you. Right by your side." She kissed him lightly. "I can't believe you asked that."

"That's how we started, and you were the one

who insisted that great sex didn't mean we were meant for a lifetime.''

''That was before I got to really know you. And we're doing that now, aren't we? Shooting for the lifetime?''

His smile was slow in coming. ''Oh, yeah.''

''You have to be the gentlest man I've ever known, which contradicts your profession, you know.''

''You made me this way, baby.''

She shook her head. ''If anything, Juliana did.''

He smiled, all papa proud. ''Yeah. She is something.''

She laid her head on his shoulder, hugging him. ''So's her daddy,'' Melanie said. ''He's a knight you know. Sir Galahad. Maybe you've heard of him?''

Jack laughed to himself. A man would never have to worry about his ego or pride around Melanie. He felt like a king in her arms. He felt loved and wanted. And Jack already knew that he'd fallen madly in love with Melanie.

And he was worried that because he didn't tell her he was a bastard, the little lie would tear them apart and destroy her trust.

Sarah Beauchamp was a tall leggy blonde from California married to a lieutenant commander in the Navy, who was a fighter pilot with the Navy squadrons attached to the Marine Air Group 31 in the area. Sarah was a civilian OR nurse and the head of the Naval Ombudsman Association, a job that, coupled with wife and nurse, seemed monumental to Melanie. Sarah had been adding bits to the conversation, but right now was enthralled with Juliana, whom she was holding.

Beside Sarah, wearing chic slacks and a blouse, was Sue Bradshaw, the LINKS team leader, who was married to a marine gunnery sergeant in Force Recon. While her son, Shawn, was having a blast on the gym set, Sue's husband, Gary, was on the other side of the yard standing at the grill with Jack and Sarah's husband, Daniel. Maria, a black-haired Hispanic woman who seemed to know every answer to every question, sat next to Melanie. She was a former Marine, though at first glance, she was the last person Melanie would have expected to carry a weapon and shout "oo-rah." Maria was head of the Marine Key Volunteer Program for two bases in the area. The women were a font of information, yet after about ten minutes of talking in abbreviations and acronyms, they had Melanie's head swimming.

"Okay, let's see, BX means Base Exchange, PX means Post Exchange," Melanie said.

"Yeah, Post is Army talk," Maria said, "and practically blasphemous."

Melanie smiled. "MP means Military Police, MWR means Morale Welfare and Recreation, and that includes child-care centers, BX bowling alley, gyms, shops, theaters." She stopped. "So what's TMO?"

"Traffic Management Office. Those are the household-goods supervisors, freight shipping, passenger travel, all on orders. They're the people who'll organize the moves for you."

"They do it all?"

Sue laughed softly. "No, they don't. You have to

fill out paperwork until you are blue in the face, but they do great things like come by and inspect the movers in action. Take action if anything is damaged or improperly packed.''

"And sometimes you do it all yourself if your husband is out of the country," Maria said. "My husband is deployed right now."

"I can do that."

"Good, because with Jack's MOS—method of service," Sarah clarified, "you'll likely do it at least once alone." Sarah crossed her legs and bounced Juliana on the top of her foot.

Melanie was learning more in one afternoon than she thought she could in a year. They brought her booklets and actual books on how to be an officer's wife, books about protocol, relocation packets and change of duty. Services. She'd be reading for a week, she thought, feeling overwhelmed.

"Hey, Singer, do you need a Marine to show you how to cook that steak?" Sue called out.

"The Navy can handle it," Jack said. "Anyway, we have a Marine, though I don't know what good he's doing."

"I'm reminding you when to flip the steak," Sue's husband said.

The four men growled out "Hoo-yah" and "Ooh-rah."

"Oh, Lord, the testosterone level is hitting new heights," Sarah said, cuddling Juliana, then looking for permission from Melanie before she offered the baby a cookie to gnaw on.

"Ask and you shall receive," Maria said. "If I

don't know the answer or Sarah doesn't, then we know who can give it to you."

"And come to LINKS," Sue said. "It teaches you how to be a military wife. Sometime the service member thinks either we don't need to know or we already do know after one coffee klatch or a chat in the commissary."

Collectively they rolled their eyes in agreement.

"The one thing is that Jack's a SEAL, which means that more or less the wives are on the need-to-know basis," Sarah said. "SEAL actions are classified, so don't expect to learn where he's been and what he's doing. It's the same with Force Recon."

Sue leaned forward and said, "And they'll debate for years about which is the more macho, Recon or SEALs. I never add my two cents. I like my Navy friends too much." She patted Melanie's arm.

"Oh, forewarned," Melanie said, smiling.

"When they are deployed, there's a chain of command for information. Because I'm the Key Volunteer, I get it straight from the colonel and the sergeant major. My job is to keep the spouse informed and stop nasty rumors," Maria said.

"Same here," Sarah said.

"How do you get over the fear?" Mel asked.

"You don't," Sue said. "You live with it. Your job—our job—is to make certain when our men go into battle, they won't worry about home and family and they'll know you'll be okay. Learn to handle anything they throw at you and do it in a—"

"—proficient military fashion," the rest of the women joined to say.

Melanie laughed. "Okay, as long as I can call on you all, I'm content."

"Good." Almost in unison, they set aside the paperwork and books and leaned in.

"Daniel's known Jack since the academy," Sarah said. "And I know Gary and Jack served together, but neither of them will say doing what. So how did you meet Jack?"

Melanie glanced over at Jack. "His sister is my best friend. She was my pledge to the sorority. I'd heard a lot about him, but had never met him until two weeks before Lisa married."

"It must have been awful learning you were pregnant when he couldn't be reached."

Melanie had been up front with the women, especially when Jack announced to their husbands that he was married with a child. "It wasn't pleasant, but I dealt with it."

"True Navy-wife material," Sue said. "My husband wasn't around for one of my pregnancies. Left when I wasn't even showing and arrived home three days after I'd had our second child. I wasn't exactly feeling frisky, if you know what I mean."

Melanie smiled again, admiring them and wondering how they survived so well. She wanted to be a valuable part of this elite group of women, as she was, by virtue of marriage. They were strong and resourceful and giving. She looked over at Jack, suddenly thinking about more children and years down the road with him. She'd been on birth control since Juliana was born, but the thought of having another child didn't scare her as she'd thought it would. She had some of the burdens to share. Well, all of them to share, she corrected.

"Oh, I remember that look," Sarah said, when Melanie didn't take her eyes off Jack. He was smiling at her, his gaze doing that lazy prowl over her that made her feel beautiful and desired and possessed. She wanted to be possessed. Because Jack did it in the best way.

"Catch all you can now, honey," Sue said. "We have to make it last through tough times."

Melanie stood and walked to Jack. The other men backed up a bit, offering a greeting, but Melanie slid her arms around Jack and kissed him.

The group howled with applause.

Jack caught his breath and said, "What's that for?"

"Thanks for inviting them, Jack," she whispered.

"I thought an introduction from the ladies would be clearer than hearing it all from me."

"Oh, it is." She eased back, but he kept his arm around her waist. "Now," she said, looking at the men. "I want to know how come the Marines are a part of the Navy?"

Gary spoke up. "We need someone to sail us to the war."

Good-natured laughter erupted, and Melanie thought she might be afraid for Jack, but she would be well taken care of—her family had just grown so much bigger.

Eleven

It was official. She had an ID card with the most dreadful picture of herself ever, stickers on her car, and she could actually speak in acronyms and abbreviations, like IPAC, Cencom, SecNav, and know what they meant. In the back of her heart, she felt she was destined for this. She soaked it up like a sponge. Jack had shown her the local base, and although they were Marine installations, he wanted her to get the feel of it, be aware of passing by armed guards, security checks and know the territory that was off-limits, as well as all the facilities. He'd answered her questions patiently, and she felt her excitement build. Life with him was going to be an adventure. She was looking forward to it. Which surprised her.

"You need to stop grinning to yourself," Lisa said. "People are gonna talk."

Melanie swung her gaze to Lisa's and smiled. Juliana was in bed, Jack was off helping Sarah's husband put in a dog fence at their quarters, and she and Lisa had enjoyed a good hour of cappuccino and catching up on their friendship.

"You stop in the middle of a conversation and just grin," Lisa said.

"Yeah, so?"

"Lord, you sound like Jack," Lisa said with a laugh.

Melanie frowned questioningly.

"He can't stop talking about you two, the future, and he does that same—" Lisa gestured meaninglessly "—face thing you do."

"And your point is?"

Lisa's eyes widened. "You're in love with my brother, aren't you? Despite everything that got you here, you fell in love with him."

"Yes," Melanie admitted. "I did."

"Have you told him?"

"No."

"Why not?"

"Because I'd thought I was in love before and it came back to bite me."

"Jack loves you."

Melanie rolled her eyes and knew she shouldn't have said anything. Lisa was just as bullheaded as Jack. "You're prejudiced."

"No, honest. I know he's in love with you."

"He said that?"

"No, but it's the face thing. We sisters know when they're guilty, too."

"Oh, really. How so?"

"Don't try to change the subject. You're scared."

"Sure I am. We're married—it's lifelong in my book."

"So you think you're going to go through, say, thirty years of marriage and never say the words to him?"

"No." Melanie looked down at her coffee cup. "He didn't marry me because he wanted to, Lisa, and I'm having a hard time believing what he's feeling. He was doing the right thing in his mind."

"Oh, Melanie," Lisa said sympathetically. "He'd love you without Juliana."

"He married me because of her."

"And how do you think he feels, marrying a woman who did everything she could *not* to say I do. He could have just married you and gone back to work. Or never showed up at all."

"I know."

Lisa frowned. "You don't trust him."

"I trust Jack, the man. Feelings are another subject. He was so adamant about marriage, almost fanatical. Like it was the only solution."

"For Jack it was."

Melanie opened her mouth to agree, then she focused on Lisa's expression. It was almost sad.

"Jack's honorable, and it means a lot to him for his child to have his name."

"It was more than that."

Lisa hesitated for half a minute. "That's because of his father."

Melanie frowned. "He loved his father. He talks about David all the time."

"David was my father, not Jack's."

"I don't get it."

"That's because I was born a bastard," came the response from the doorway, and Melanie looked up as Jack entered the kitchen through the garage. He set his new toolbox, which no longer looked new, on the floor.

Lisa got up to prepare a small pot of coffee.

Jack winked at her, assuring Lisa that she hadn't done anything she shouldn't have. He didn't think she believed him. "Lisa and I have the same mother, not the same father," he said to Melanie. "My father skipped out on Mom when she was pregnant with me. So she raised me alone until she met David."

Lisa grabbed her purse and, whispering that the coffee was on, said goodbye to Melanie and quietly slipped out.

Melanie only nodded, her gaze on her husband.

"So you see, Melanie, I know what it's like being called a bastard to my face."

"Why didn't you tell me this?"

"You didn't want to marry me in the first place, and I figured you would think my own illegitimacy wasn't reason enough to marry me."

"Your lineage doesn't matter to me, Jack."

Jack's mouth quirked in a smile. He should have known. "When my mom fell in love with David, I was a happy kid. He treated me like his own and adopted me, so I had his last name. He was the greatest father in the world." Jack smiled to himself, missing the heck out of David and thinking he could use his advice right now. "Then they gave me a sister to tease."

Melanie realized that though Jack might be telling

this casually, it meant a great deal to him. He looked at Melanie, his eyes hardening. "I lived for a few years with the stigma, and it wasn't pleasant. Not till David changed everything. I remember being called names, but it was the judging looks from adults that hurt the most." He moved toward her, gripping her shoulders and staring down into her beautiful eyes. "Juliana won't have anyone but us, and I couldn't stand that everyone would think her father didn't have the guts to marry her mother. Or that he didn't care about her."

Melanie looked down, feeling her heart moving on shaky ground. "I see."

He tipped her chin up, dread crashing through him at the tears in her eyes. "Oh, honey, I didn't mean to keep that from you this long."

"But you did, when I've been honest with you."

"Were you?"

"Of course I was. I've told you how I felt."

"Sure, about everything except what's in your heart."

As if he'd discovered some secret, she curled away, breaking his hold. "And what have you said, Jack, other than the same thing all along—'I want marriage for her sake.' I actually feel jealous of my own child because she had your heart first."

He reached for her. "Melanie—"

The phone rang. Jack snatched it up, about to bark at the caller before he took a breath and said hello. He listened, and Melanie watched his expression grow more serious, harsher. He grunted at the caller and hung up.

"That was Reese," he said. "I have to report back in two days."

"Two? But you still have a few days' leave left."

"Not anymore. This means I have to leave tomorrow morning for Virginia."

Damn, Melanie thought. Panic swept her. Oh, damn.

She stared at him, angry with him, with herself for distrusting her heart, and wanting him just to hold her.

Her continued silence cut him. "I have to pack," he said, and moved past her toward the bedroom.

"Let me give you a hand."

"No, it won't take long. I travel light."

She felt a door shut between them, and she wasn't going to let that happen. "Jack," she called, following him into the bedroom. He already had a duffel bag on the bed. "Stop."

He stilled, clothes in his hands, and looked at her with cool eyes. He was mad. Or just irritated with her?

"You can't leave like this."

"I have to. This is what it means to be in the service."

"Dammit, you know what I'm talking about. Jeez, why do I feel guilty all of a sudden?"

"You figure it out."

"You're the one who lied."

"No, I just didn't tell you I was a bastard. I was, frankly, ashamed of it."

"Oh, honey, you shouldn't be. It's not your fault."

"Right, and I wasn't going to make my father's mistake with my daughter."

"Yes, sure," she snapped. "Marry the mom and make *you* feel better." She wished the words back the instant they left her mouth.

He glared at her, hurt glittering in his blue eyes. "You know that's not true, dammit."

"I'm sorry, I do, but—"

Juliana began to cry, and when Melanie went to get her, Jack moved past Melanie, saying he would. She let him go, wondering what she was doing to them right now and thinking herself foolish. The phone rang a few minutes later. She answered it and then went to the nursery, where he sat with the baby in his arms and a solemn look on his face.

"It's Reese again."

Jack took the phone from her. "Yeah, okay fine," he said into the receiver after a moment. He checked his watch. "No, I'll be there." He shut the phone off, handing it back to her.

Melanie clutched it to her chest.

"They have a Marine transport plane leaving from the Air Station, headed to Virginia, and room on it for me."

"What's that mean?"

"I leave tonight. At midnight."

Melanie sighed and nodded. Her two days just turned into a few hours.

Well, she'd expected this. He'd warned her. She stared at the phone in her hand and swore she wasn't going to make a scene. What had Maria said? It was her job to be strong so he didn't have to worry. She swallowed and when he whispered her name, she met his gaze.

Jack's heart shattered right then. "Come here," he

said, and she flew to him, trapping him against her. Juliana snuggled herself against her father's chest and grabbed a lock of her mom's hair.

Jack pressed his lips to Melanie's temple. He didn't want to leave. God, not now.

Melanie cooked as though she expected Jack never to eat again. He was amused and didn't have the heart to tell her he wasn't really hungry—not for food, anyway. But the meal eased the tension between them, and he hated that she was hurting. She wasn't alone in her pain, and when Juliana was in her crib for the night, Jack struggled with the goodbye he didn't want to say, knowing the baby wouldn't miss him that much, since she was so young. Then he stowed his gear by the door, pressed and laid out his uniform and glanced at the clock. He felt like a man about to go to execution if he didn't confess. And his salvation was with Melanie.

He walked into the bedroom. She stood in the shadows, moonlight falling over, missing in spots, showing her beauty in others. Without a word she crossed to him, wrapped her arms around him and kissed him hungrily.

His knees softened with the force behind her kiss, and Jack needed nothing more than the freedom his heart felt when he was holding her. In moments their clothes lay scattered on the floor, and their bodies naked and hot and clinging to feel more and more. The desperation in them magnified each movement. Each touch had power, like needles of heat sinking into their skin.

In her mind Melanie couldn't let him go. In a

small place she refused to acknowledge, she understood that this could be the last time she touched him.

And Jack knew it. It made his throat constrict. They had a couple of hours, no more. And both wondered if it would be their last together.

Melanie poured herself into every kiss, adored him with every keening breath. She left her imprint on him, claiming him completely. He tasted her flesh like a man about to be imprisoned. To him he was. Separated from Melanie would be madness. It was already creeping in, and then, unable to temper his need, unable to think of anything but proving the feelings spilling through his heart, he pulled her beneath him, held her as he pushed her thighs apart and possessed her. She flexed beautifully, a smooth lush arch, and Jack thrust into her, his fingers laced with hers as he slid back and then pushed home. He watched her face, saw love shining there and wished she'd speak of it. He loved her so damn much his insides came apart with the thought of losing her, with the very idea that she couldn't trust her heart to him. She was scared of being hurt. So was he. But he took the risk and let himself love her at first sight. There was no turning back. Never had been.

Emotions and movements blended. When he touched, his actions spoke of his love for her. She responded with soft moans and sweet smiles, and then she gave back to him. In simple ways, such as a kiss, a stroke of her fingers through his hair, the way her hips lifted now to greet him.

Their loving was tender and patient, though time was their enemy. He challenged it, wanting her totally, wanting everything, selfishly, greedily. With her gaze locked to his, he watched the exquisite fire of her climax rise and rise. He shoved and the passion broke, splintering, then flowing through them like hot, red wine.

They clung together madly, fingertips digging, bodies fused, and even after the haze settled round them like a soft blanket, they kept their bodies tightly woven in a tangle of arms and legs.

Jack lifted his head, kissing her before he whispered, "I'm going to miss you, baby."

Melanie felt her heart crack. "Oh, Jack. I hate that you're leaving. I know you have to, I accept that, but I can barely stand it."

"Me neither." His gaze searched hers, his fingers pushing the damp hair off her face. "I didn't think it would be this hard." *Because I love you,* he thought.

"You'll be back soon. I'll keep busy. I'll look for a place in Virginia."

He kissed her again and glanced at the clock.

"I have to get showered."

She nodded, and when he moved off her and slipped from the bed, she turned her back on him, not wanting him to see her cry.

Lisa had come over to sit with Juliana while Jack and Melanie went to the airstrip. Melanie glanced at Jack as he returned the sentry's salute and drove through the airfield gates. Jack was wearing a khaki uniform, his chest covered in too many ribbons and gold emblems for one so young, she thought. What had he done to earn them? How many more would he earn and she'd never know what for?

Her breath shuddered through her. He pulled onto the flight line, parked her car and climbed out. Carrying his bags, he walked with Melanie to the hangar. She was awed by the size of it, the noise level high. Jack didn't say anything except salute Marines before they came to the huge open doors.

A wide gray aircraft was several yards away, a group of Marines loading cargo into it.

A young Marine wearing red headphones trotted up to Jack, stopped and snapped a sharp salute. Jack returned it.

"Ma'am," he said, touching his fingertips to the brim of his camouflage cover. Melanie nodded and tried to smile.

The Marine looked at Jack, his gaze dropping briefly to the SEAL emblem on his chest. "Glad to have you aboard, sir." He gestured to the duffel. "I can stow that for you if you'd like some more time with your lady, sir."

Jack nodded, handing over the bag. The Marine spun around and trotted back to the plane.

Jack looked at Melanie. "I have to get on board. Hate to have them dogging me because I held up the flight."

Melanie bit her lip, refusing to embarrass him with tears. But with each passing second she felt she was being drained of life.

His lips quirked in a smile. "This is about the only time I'm allowed to kiss you in public, you know."

She smiled weakly. "No public displays of affection, I know."

He held her gaze, his blue eyes going dark with emotion. He brushed a kiss to her lips and whispered, "I love you, Melanie." Then he turned and walked away.

She blinked and swallowed. "Don't you drop a bomb like that and think you can walk away, Singer."

He stopped, but didn't turn around.

"You really love me?"

He turned, and with an unreadable expression, strode back to her, gathered her in his arms and kissed her senseless. Absolutely senseless.

"Yes, I really do." He scraped her hair back off her face and cupped her jaw. His gaze was dark and intense. "You've been in my mind and heart from that first day, Melanie. Sure I love our daughter, but I loved you first. *You.* Because you're still the woman who knocked me over at my sister's wedding. That's the woman I fell in love with."

Melanie stared into his ice-blue eyes and saw only cool calm seas. The distrust and fear she held unwound like a velvet ribbon. Her heart no longer struggled and the words tumbled off her lips. "Oh, Jack," she whispered, "I love you, too."

His grin was slow and wide. "About time you said it."

"Excuse me?"

She gave him an affronted look and he laughed softly. "I knew you did. You were just too scared to say it."

Her anger left her before it had the chance to boil. "You're right, I was scared. I've been so happy these past weeks that I was terrified it wasn't real, that I wanted it so badly that I couldn't trust what I already knew. But it doesn't matter. Scared is okay. Fear keeps you sharp." She repeated his own words back at him. "Nothing, not even fear or our being apart is going to ever change my love for you, Jack Singer." Now she cupped his face, her confession giving her the freedom she'd always wanted. "Not the date on a license or certificate, either. It doesn't matter how we started this marriage, only how we live it."

The plane's engine revved.

"Oh, Jack."

"I love you, Melanie. I was a goner the moment you called me Sir Galahad."

She grinned through a teary smile. "My hero," she said, and he kissed her deeply.

The Marines watching them hung out of the transport, howling like Comanche raiders. Someone called out and the engine noise grew louder.

"I have to go."

"Go then. I'll be here. I'll hold down the fort, waiting for you to come home to me."

He brushed her lips with his fingers and stole one more kiss.

"This time and forever, Jack."

Jack's chest locked with emotion, and defying the pilot's orders to get aboard, Jack grabbed her and kissed her again, then let her go and walked to the plane, happiness lighting his face.

Once inside, he gripped a strap, then looked back to see her smiling. A smile that lit her entire body and shouted back at him, *I love you!*

Then just before the hydraulic door stole her from his sight, she yelled, "Hoo-yahh!"

Lt. Jack Singer, U.S. Navy SEAL, would always

remember this moment as the day Melanie brought him to his knees with her declaration.

A surprise baby had given him the love of his lifetime. His soul knew it the first time he saw Melanie. And nothing was ever going to keep him from having the pleasure of proving it to her for the rest of her life.

Epilogue

Three years later

Jack stepped into the kitchen. Melanie didn't look at all pleased and Juliana was sitting in a chair pouting and sniffling.

He set his briefcase down and said, "Hey, what's up?"

Melanie spun around, then came over to him and kissed him.

"Hi, Daddy," Juliana said sullenly.

"Hey, princess."

Melanie said clearly, "We've had a difference of opinion. I thought she shouldn't be messing with the scissors, and she thought she could give herself a haircut."

Jack groaned, just now noticing that Juliana's hair

was much shorter. He squatted down in front of his daughter. "Oh, man." He touched the shortened locks. He eyed her darkly.

"I'm sorry," his little girl blubbered, her lip quivering, and Jack felt himself about to cave.

Melanie cleared her throat, and when he looked at her, she inclined her head. Jack knew better than to go soft on his daughter right now. Even when she stared at him with those soulful blue eyes.

"I want you to think about what disobeying me has cost you, honey." Melanie hated punishing Juliana. "Go to your room."

Juliana slipped off the chair and clomped toward her room.

As soon as she was gone, Melanie's face broke into a smile. "You should have seen the haircut. Thank heaven that Dara next door is a hairdresser. I was about to scalp that child with a Marine regulation high and tight I was so mad."

Laughing, Jack crossed to her. "Anyway I can ease the tension?" He wrapped his arms around her.

"Yeah, you can." She sighed into his arms, feeling his strength and drawing it into her. "I want chocolate and a bubble bath."

"Easy enough."

He kissed her warmly, wanting more and wondering if their daughter would stay in her room as she was told. He'd only just returned from a short deployment a couple of weeks ago, and he and Melanie still had some catching up to do.

They parted and she went to the stove, stirring a pot of homemade soup. Jack let his gaze wander over her. Every day he thanked God for that night after his sister's wedding.

"Can you come over to the Command tomorrow at nine?" He snatched a carrot from the cutting board and munched.

"Sure, why?"

"I'd like you to pin on my oak leaves."

She whipped around, her eyes wide. "You got the promotion!"

He just grinned and her smile went hundred-watt bright.

"Oh, Jack!" Melanie dropped the spoon and launched herself at him, jumping into his arms and wrapping her legs around his waist. "I'm so proud of you!"

Jack laughed and didn't think he could feel any better, but he did. "Is this the behavior of the wife of a lieutenant commander?"

"Have I ever been politically correct?" She kissed him hard and met his gaze. "This is so great. And we'll need the money."

He frowned. "Anything specific you have in mind?"

"Saving for two college educations."

He just stared at her.

She tipped her head to the side and said, "You know for a lieutenant commander selectee you're slow on the uptake."

His eyes flew wide. "We're pregnant."

She smiled. "If you want to have this baby, I'll see if it can be arranged."

"Oh, Lord," he said softly, and swung her into his arms, then sank into a chair.

"Happy?"

"Yes!" He rained kisses over her face, squeezing her. He was going to get the chance to see her pregnant, and although he'd viewed the videotape and had seen the pictures of her last delivery, it was not the same as being there. Thoughts of putting in for a SEAL-instructor position for a while popped into his mind.

"We might get a boy this time."

He lifted his gaze to hers, and Melanie was unhinged by the look in his eyes.

"I don't care."

A woman couldn't ask for more, she thought. Jack never failed to surprise her. "I love you, Jack."

"I love you, too, baby," he murmured, and stood up with her in his arms, carrying her from the kitchen into the living room and settling comfortably on the sofa. He never let her go. "How do you feel?"

"Ask me in the morning," she said, grinning. "This promotion means orders, doesn't it?"

"Yes, very likely."

"To where?"

He shrugged. "California. Maybe West PAC."

She waved off the Navy installations he suggested, not really caring where they went, as long as they were together. "When?"

"A few weeks to a few months."

Hurry up and wait, she thought, and looked around at their darling house and all the work she'd put into it. Oh, well, she thought and sighed into his arms.

His hand slid down to her belly, slipping under the band of her jeans, his palm warm and teasing on her skin. She studied his expression, the awe in it, and was glad she'd get to experience this baby with him near this time.

"I want to know everything," he told her.

"Oh, swollen ankles, barfing at the crack of dawn…oh, so sexy," she said.

His expression remained serious. "It is to me, Melanie. Everything about you is."

"Daddy," his daughter called from the hallway.

Melanie arched a brow.

"Yes, Juliana," he said in a tone that reminded her that he was not pleased with her behavior this afternoon.

"Can I come out?"

He looked at Melanie. She nodded.

"Sure, honey."

Juliana stepped around the corner, her eyes red-rimmed and downcast.

"Come on, munchkin," Melanie said, and her daughter leapt onto the sofa, instantly snuggling up to her father and mother.

Melanie didn't tell her that she was going to have a brother or sister. She'd save it for later and savor the private knowledge with Jack a bit longer. She lifted her gaze to his, touching the side of his face. Gently he kissed her, whispered his love, then looked down at Juliana.

While Jack bestowed one of his lessons about disobedience on their daughter, Melanie shifted into the cushions, listening, watching the way Juliana looked at her father with complete trust and adoration.

Melanie smiled, thinking of the new life inside her, the new branch of strength that would be her family. In her arms was all she loved. All that mattered to her. They'd travel the world together, face whatever the Navy threw their way. Jack called them his homeport, his anchor, when in reality, they were hers.

Long ago Melanie had admitted that she'd been lost to the pain in her heart, filled with distrust and sinking fast. Then Jack stepped through the door. Her future had started with a velvety look and a wonderful man in Navy dress whites.

Sir Galahad had definitely ridden to the rescue that night, she thought, and he'd stolen away with her heart.

* * * * *

Silhouette® **Desire**®

presents

DYNASTIES:
THE
CONNELLYS

A brand-new miniseries about the Connellys of Chicago,
a wealthy, powerful American family tied by blood to the
royal family of the island kingdom of Altaria.
They're wealthy, powerful and rocked by
scandal, betrayal…and passion!

Look for a whole year of glamorous and
utterly romantic tales in 2002:

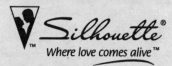

Silhouette®

Where love comes alive™

$ Saving Money $
Has Never Been
This Easy!

Just fill out and send in this form from any
October, November and December 2002 books
and we will send you a coupon booklet worth a
total savings of $20.00 off future purchases of
Harlequin and Silhouette books in 2003.

Yes! It's that easy!

**I accept your incredible offer!
Please send me a coupon booklet:**

Name (PLEASE PRINT)

Address   Apt. #

City   State/Prov.   Zip/Postal Code

**In a typical month, how many
Harlequin and Silhouette novels do you read?**

❑ 0-2   ❑ 3+

097KJKDNC7   097KJKDNDP

Please send this form to:
   In the U.S.: Harlequin Books, P.O. Box 9071, Buffalo, NY 14269-9071
   In Canada: Harlequin Books, P.O. Box 609, Fort Erie, Ontario L2A 5X3

Allow 4-6 weeks for delivery. Limit one coupon booklet per household. Must be
postmarked no later than January 15, 2003.

PHQ402

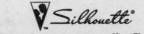

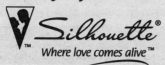

COMING NEXT MONTH

#1471 All in the Game—Barbara Boswell

She had come to an island paradise as a reality game show contestant. But Shannen Cullen hadn't expected to come face-to-face with the man who had broken her heart nine years ago. Sexy Tynan Howe was back, and wreaking havoc on Shannen's emotions. She was falling in love with him all over again, but could she trust him?

#1472 Expecting…and in Danger—Eileen Wilks

Dynasties: The Connellys

They had been lovers—for a night. Now, five months later, Charlotte Masters was pregnant and on the run. When Rafe Connelly found her, he proposed a marriage of convenience. Because she was wary of her handsome protector, she refused, yet nothing could have prepared her for the healing—and passion—that awaited her in his embrace….

#1473 Delaney's Desert Sheikh—Brenda Jackson

Sheikh Jamal Ari Yasir had come to his friend's cabin for some rest and relaxation. But his plans were turned upside down when sassy Delaney Westmoreland arrived. Though they agreed to stay out of each other's way, they eventually gave in to their undeniable attraction. Yet when his vacation ended, would Jamal do his duty and marry the woman his family had chosen, or would he follow his heart?

#1474 Taming the Prince—Elizabeth Bevarly

Crown and Glory

Shane Cordello was more than just strong muscles and a handsome face— he was also next in line for the throne of Penwyck. Then, as Shane and his escort, Sara Wallington, were en route to Penwyck, their plane was hijacked. And as the danger surrounding them escalated, so did their passion. But upon their return, could Sara transform the royal prince into a willing husband?

#1475 A Lawman in Her Stocking—Kathie DeNosky

Vowing not to have her heart broken again, Brenna Montgomery moved to Texas to start a new life—only to find her vow tested when her matchmaking grandmother introduced her to gorgeous Dylan Chandler. The handsome sheriff made her ache with desire, but could he also heal her battered heart?

#1476 Do You Take This Enemy?—Sara Orwig

Stallion Pass

When widowed rancher Gabriel Brant disregarded a generations-old family feud and proposed a marriage of convenience to beautiful—and pregnant— Ashley Ryder, he did so because it was an arrangement that would benefit both of them. But his lovely bride stirred his senses, and he soon found himself falling under her spell. Somehow Gabe had to show Ashley that he could love, honor and cherish her—forever!

SDCNM1002